Index of Stories & Poetry:

Ink Monkey Magazine

Ink Monkey Magazine

Ink Monkey Magazine

Ink Monkey Magazine

Ink Monkey Magazine

Ink Monkey Magazine

Ink Monkey Magazine

Ink Monkey Magazine

Ink Monkey Magazine

Ink Monkey Magazine

Ink Monkey Magazine

Ink Monkey Magazine

Ink Monkey Magazine

Ink Monkey Magazine

Ink Monkey Magazine

Ink Monkey Magazine

Ink Monkey Magazine

Starting with issue four (that's this one), we at Ink Monkey Mag decided that it's a lot of work to do a project such as this one. Because of that, we decided to bring on a guest editor from now on. We would like to welcome *Linda Silvey* as our inaugural guest editor.

I have been familiar with Linda's work for many years now, and if I could only write half as well as she does, I'd be far better off than I already am. For more on Linda, check out her story (page 43), or check out her extended biography on our website.

Ink Monkey Magazine – Issue 4

© **2010 Ink Monkey Press. All Rights Reserved.**

She reeked of boredom. Summer in Knoxville is not the place to be.

"Herbal Tea? We only have tea or sweet tea."

"What is sweet tea?"

"Tea that is sweet."

My Southern California experience with tea was the murky variety with chunks of acidic wood bark. Drinking it reflected the suffocating Los Angeles mind-set of being a rail thin, narcissistic, high-class hippie.

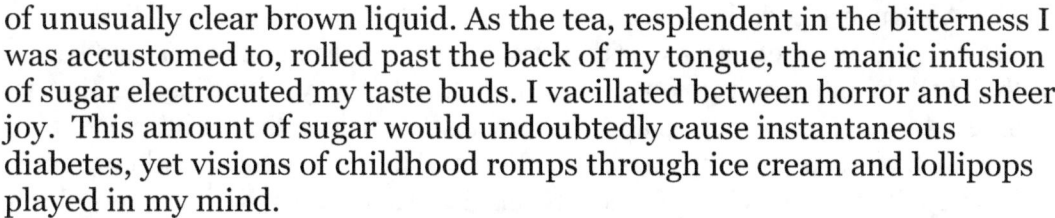

Sweet Tea

Kehaunani Hubbard

I was handed a tumbler of unusually clear brown liquid. As the tea, resplendent in the bitterness I was accustomed to, rolled past the back of my tongue, the manic infusion of sugar electrocuted my taste buds. I vacillated between horror and sheer joy. This amount of sugar would undoubtedly cause instantaneous diabetes, yet visions of childhood romps through ice cream and lollipops played in my mind.

"Mom, what's wrong?" My six-year-old daughter looked worried.

I felt my pupils dilate and with a chipmunk voice I sputtered, "Nothing's wrong, honey. I feel wonderful! Does my voice sound funny? Do my eyes look weird?!"

I had been existing on an emotional diet of numbness and tears since my husband's death four weeks ago. This trip to Tennessee was a trial run to see if we would fit in with the South. Savannah wisely questioned my sudden bliss. Several minutes later, calmness from my sugar crash settled into my belly and I took a deep, honest breath. I realized I had two options; stick to lumber water, mimicking my LA past, or loosen my belt and move to Tennessee.

Kehaunani Hubbard is an essayist working on her memoir.
She lives in Nashville, TN with her daughter.

Convergence
EC Jarvis

A sequence is defined as a function (not a "series of numbers," that would confuse later definitions) with a first number, a second number, and so forth for all the integers from one to infinity. Another way of putting it is that an infinite sequence of numbers is a function whose domain is the set of integers greater than or equal to some integer n_o. Some of these sequences will converge, and some will diverge. Convergence means that each successive term gets closer and closer to some number. Divergence means that the sequence never settles on a single number.

***

We were both in the classroom early. There were one or two of our classmates there, but most of the seats were open, so I sat in Laura's general vicinity. She was looking at the textbook and tapping her lips. When I sat down, she briefly looked over at me and gave a fraction of a smile.

"What do you think of this class so far?" I said.

She looked over at me. "It's all right so far, I guess. Little early to tell."

"Mhm. The professor can be a little long winded."

There was a slight downturn in Laura's lips after I said this. "I think he's all right. I don't know any of the profs, but one of my friends who goes here recommended him to me, actually."

I nodded and began to study my own textbook. If she didn't know any profs, then, she might well be a freshman like myself, and this could indicate that she would be single, again, like myself. If she did not want to be attached when heading off to college, it would be likely she'd be available at this early point in the semester.

***

A series is the sum of the terms of a sequence. So, if you add up all the terms in a sequence, you have a series. Even if a sequence converges, its corresponding series can still diverge. A sequence converging is a necessary condition, but not sufficient one for proving a series converges. Take, for instance, a sequence where every term is one, clearly, that sequence converges to one. However, if you add up an infinite number of ones, you will go off to infinity. Your sum will be amorphous and inconceivable to the human mind.

***

Through our study group, Laura and I got to see a fair amount of each other. A typical session might go something like this:

Laura: Number 23 converges.

Group member #2: Converges, or converges absolutely?

Me: Just converges. Use the comparison test, then the integral test.

(Various mutterings of other group members.)

Me: (To Laura) What did you end up doing last weekend?

Laura: I just stayed in and watched a movie with my roommates.

Me: Nobody wanted to go out?

Laura: One of my roommate's friends called, but I didn't feel like going out with him. I think she's trying to set us up.

Me: But you're not interested.

Group member #1: Compare it to one over root 2n?

Laura: Root 3n. Root 2n would actually be less. You want to show it diverges.

Group member #1: Oh. right.

Me: But you're not interested?

Laura: No, I'm not too into him. Did you do anything exciting?

Me: No.

***

If a series has no negative terms, one can use the comparison test to prove whether the series converges or diverges. The comparison test involves, first, a conjecture, if one assumes the series *converges*, then one finds a larger sequence known to converge, proving that the series in question, being smaller, *must* converge. Conversely, if one assumes the series in question *diverges*, then one finds a smaller sequence known to diverge. Thus, although one will not find the actual sum of a given series, one at least can determine whether or not a finite sum exists. Sometimes, this is the best for which one can hope.

***

After one of the group sessions, I walked Laura to the bus stop. There was an elderly man waiting for the bus. He sat silently and didn't look directly at us. She and I were discussing a future session. "Maybe this weekend we could get together and look it over?" I asked.

She bit her lower lip. "I don't know. I kind of like my weekends to be weekends, you know?"

I looked down.

"That doesn't necessarily mean that you and I can't do anything this weekend. Just maybe not math."

This response was even in excess of my expectations. "That sounds great."

I took her hands and gave a slight squeeze. We smiled at each other, there in the dim light of the bus stop, and we even kissed. Imagine what the old man must have told whoever passed for his friends about us.

I asked her if she wanted me to wait with her for the bus, but she said she'd be fine, and that I should go. I already had her phone number for study-group purposes (easy to remember, the last four digits were a Pythagorean triple given the proper placement of commas), so we kissed once more, and I was off.

***

You can express the concept of convergence graphically with a line and a number of points. The points may get closer and closer to the line from above, from below, or alternating. They may poke above and below the line, never quite touching, but always getting closer. Always approaching that stable mark. You might think of the points as straddling that line. Or jumping over it. Becoming more and more standard while still moving.

***

Let me try to describe her. Laura has blonde hair; she also has green eyes, nice, high cheek bones, and a trim figure. Not emaciated, but slender. The only real abnormality of her physical appearance is a tiny discoloration on the side of her left nostril. Most people who see it mistake it for a small stud in the side of her nose, but it's actually a very dark birthmark. It's barely noticeable. In fact, as we spent more time together, it became just a general feature to me. Nothing to unsettle or interfere. In fact, things progressed quite well. At the end of the semester, we'd even agreed to meet for New Year's.

***

Although you can't add together infinite numbers of numbers, you can, at least, approximate the sum. Sometimes this is done by integration, which is really an artificial infinite sum. It employs mathematical formulas and

8

equivalences to come to some kind of expression, which gives the sum. The theoretical number arrived at is, oddly enough, *more* accurate than any summation which could be done by hand.

***

I wanted to wait until I was out of my parents' house to do this (for obvious reasons), so, as I was leaving town to meet Laura, I stopped at a gas station. I deliberately picked a fairly small station that would require a key to the bathroom so that I could have some privacy.

I went inside and obtained the key from the clerk, a bored looking man who referred to me as "Pal."

The bathroom was not heated, and not very well lit, but beggars can't be choosers. I brought out the nub of a carrot I had in my back pocket, a cigarette lighter, and the needle. I then tore a bit of paper towel off the dispenser over the sink and set my tools on the paper, as the sink did not look particularly sterile. Rubbing my hands together for warmth, I took a few deep breaths. When I felt ready, I picked up the lighter and needle and held the needle over the flame, to sterilize it. I then set them both back down onto the paper towel. I slid the nub of the carrot up my nose, which proved to be very uncomfortable. The needle was still a bit hot to handle effectively at that point, so I stood, looking in the mirror and trying not to sneeze. I had to sniffle enough to stop the sneeze, but not so much that the nub would wedge itself too high up my nose. I tried holding the nub and sniffling, but this was neither more effective nor more comfortable than sniffling without holding it.

Before long, my eyes began to water, and I decided that I would have to go ahead with it before I was unable to function. The needle was hot, but not unbearable. The pain as I pushed it through my nose was not as terrible as I feared it might be, but it bled a bit more than I expected it to. I pulled the needle back and forth in the hole to try widening it a bit. I let the wound bleed into the sink as I took the tiny bottle of rubbing alcohol out of my jacket pocket and folded up another piece of paper towel to soak it up.

The pain of the contact with alcohol, especially on the rough, gas-station, paper towel, was worse than the original puncture. I dabbed and wiped until it seemed to be mostly done bleeding. I threw away the needle and carrot nub, stuffed the alcohol and lighter into my jacket pockets, and went back to the gas station attendant.

Bill, as his nametag indicated, still looked bored, and either didn't notice or didn't comment upon my new feature. I did leave the bloodied paper towel on the bathroom sink, though, so I suspect he had some excitement later in his day as he tried to formulate a narrative of what must have gone on in the bathroom. Bloody paper towels, a needle (if he could find it), and a carrot nub. What would it add up to for Bill?

Different types of series and sequences will converge more quickly than others. For instance, the multiplicative inverse of the iteration's number (n_i) squared will converge, but not nearly as quickly as a geometric series will. Some series will converge at a logarithmic (slow) pace, whereas others will converge at an exponential (fast) pace. The pace of convergence is clearer further on in the series (when n is large) than it is early on (when n is 1, 2, etc.).

***

Laura and I sat down on the bed. "So," she said, "tell me how Christmas with your family was."

I told her that it had been a generally enjoyable trip, and she then told me that her Christmas had gone fairly well. Apparently a relative had flown in from somewhere to be with the family. I think it was an aunt from Maine, but I could be wrong.

It wasn't until that night that she said anything about my nose. We were laying in bed, laughing over the fact that she'd told her parents we were using separate hotel rooms (her parents tended not to be as progressive as mine), when she pulled me closer to kiss me. After the kiss, she looked at my face and asked, "What's that?"

I smiled. "I poked myself."

She bent her head back and rolled her eyes. "Well obviously. How did you do it?"

I put my arms around her and pulled her closer. "With a needle. I heated a needle and pierced my nose."

Her body went rigid in my arm. "Why would you do that?"

I quickly explained to her my decision to approximate her. "It's bringing the two of us closer together," I said. "The process of closing in on you physically brings me towards you on a number of levels."

***

A series that converges due to its terms alternating between negative and positive converges conditionally, but it may not converge absolutely. A series converges absolutely (is absolutely convergent) if and only if the corresponding series defined by the sum of the absolute value of each term converges. Converging absolutely is stronger than converging conditionally.

***

Her hand went up to her mouth and she looked away. I waited to see if that moment would bring about a union or a division. I cannot possibly convey to you the terror I felt at that moment. Much like with love and physical pain, the most intense moment with terror is that moment of anticipation. I saw a tear run down her cheek, which only confirmed my suspicions.

"Laura," I said. "It's because I love you."

She turned to me, touched my cheek with the same hand that had just been to her face, and said, "It's beautiful."

I wrapped my arms around her and kissed her. "Beautiful, like you."

She began asking me about the particulars of the operation. How long I'd been planning it, how much it hurt when I had done it. I told her about the gas station attendant, and we laughed. As we exchanged kisses, we created different scenarios together from the details I shared with her.

Laura: Were you rubbing your nose when you went back in?

Me: I imagine so. Why?

Laura: I bet he thought you were a coke fiend. You had some kind of mishap in

the bathroom.

Me: I'm on my last legs.

Laura: You've been snorting it for years, and your septum is gone.

Me: It's destroyed my career and torn apart my family.

Laura: You were heading South, trying to outrun your debt.

Me: Even in the cold, I was sweating like mad.

Laura: Just paying your bill you were about to crack.

At this point, Laura reached over and put her hand on my cheek so that her thumb touched the scab on the side of my nose. "You know," she said, "now that you've run away from your wife and kids, there's no turning back."

I reached over to touch her face so that my thumb touched her birthmark. "There's only one thing left for a desperate man to do."

Laura smiled at me. She took her hand off my face and slid it down to my chest, then to my belly. I won't go into the sordid details. I'll merely say that the two of us coupled and then stayed up to watch the ball drop at precisely midnight.

EC Jarvis has had his work in Bitter Oleander, Isotope, and other places. KNOCK nominated his work for a Pushcart Prize.

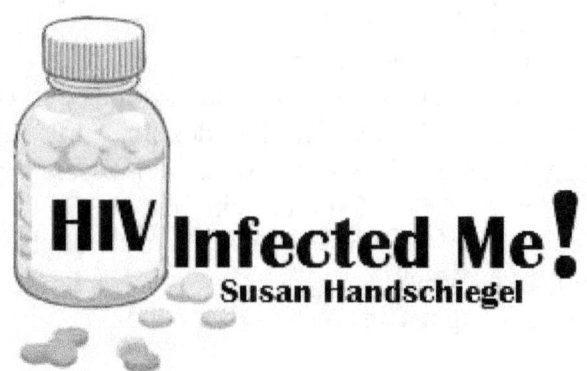

HIV Infected Me!
Susan Handschiegel

They tell me that HIV is *not* the new bubonic plague + I am being completely ridiculous for saying such an ignorant thing.

Of course, these are also the ones with good, clean blood pumping through their veins.

They are not assaulted with relentless stories of the miraculous state of Magic Johnson's t-cells.

They are not subjected to the brief flash of fear in the eyes of liberal friends who are too educated + pc to confess their disgust.

They like to chant: It's not a death sentence. It's not a death sentence.

That phrase is more worn out than a 50 year-old Hunt's Point prostitute.

More worn out than me.

Finding out that I was a hivver sucked.

I got tested, not because I thought I had it, but because I was sure I didn't.

The Chelsea Free Clinic was like the foyer of Hell. Maury Povich blared from a smeared television chained high up on the wall. A rail-thin woman yelled at her kid for putting a penny in his mouth. "That shit could hurt you," she said while punching him almost gently in the head.

My brother thought it would be funny to have me listen to Ween's "AIDS" on his Ipod. He said I was going to be just fine.

A nurse in a stained uniform called my name.

The doctor, a tiny Jamaican woman, sat me down + told me that she had really been praying that I was all right.

I guessed the blood test didn't go my way.

She had a really deep + mellow voice. A lot of that day is sort of blurry, but I *do* remember her voice.

She looked so sad when she told me that she had really been pulling for me.

She admitted to saying a prayer for me. That the result would be negative. Clearly, her relationship with God was just as one-sided + unhealthy as mine.

I lurched away from her office, barely acknowledging my brother + ex-boyfriend.

I went outside for a smoke.

They followed + I told them.

I was a hivver.

Fuck.

(Turned out the ex-boyfriend was clear. This was nice, as he had only been with 1 and a ½ women before me. Don't ask about the ½)

How was *I* supposed to know that a fiancé I had 5 years ago lied when he said he was tested every 6 months? "I have the paperwork to prove it if you're going to be such a paranoid bitch." How was *I* to know that when he said we were monogamous, he didn't count unprotected anal sex with strangers as cheating?

I had been off of heroin for about six months at this point (+ no, I never shared a needle in my life). Considering the interesting turn my life had just taken, I felt that I deserved a nice little opiate vacation.

My brother + ex insisted on accompanying me to a dealer/friend's place down on 18th Street. I wouldn't let them come inside, though. I would've hated for my brother to see the ragged company I randomly kept.

When I arrived, I was greeted with all the warmth + familiarity a shooting gallery can muster.

"Man, what are you doing here? You've been clean a minute," Matt hugged me + I cringed. I was an untouchable.

"I just got tested," I started, dramatically. "I have the Virus."

I was met with silence. Pure + unbroken.

Matt laughed. "Oh, yeah?" He gestured toward the semi-conscious lumps of his friends. "So does Steve + Jackie + Joey +, oh, see old Paul there?" An older man lifted his head from his tied up arm + smiled brokenly. "He has AIDS. Paul, you were diagnosed, when? Like, 1987?"

I don't believe that this was the reaction I had been expecting.

"Man, so what? Everyone I *know's* got the virus."

I bought a bundle of barely stepped on heroin + mumbled my gratitude.

I returned to my apartment, my brother + ex still in tow. They were convinced I was going to commit suicide. I was thinking about it.

I spent the next week nodding softly on my couch. I actually *did* have a suicide plan worked out with a friend of mine. He was going to make sure my dog was okay. Ironically, my friend died 2 days before I was going to do it. Some sort of undiagnosed + esoteric brain thing.

I decided *not* to kill myself (obviously) after his funeral. I simply cultivated a fairly mean heroin addiction for a while. Now that I think of it, I *was* sort of killing myself the lazy, Gen X way.

Ah, well.

That was 6 years ago.

So far, I'm all right. I still don't need meds – which is *awesome,* as I haven't the $5,000 for monthly doses – + I quit smack. Sometimes I still feel unclean + uncomfortable, especially around children, but most days I kind of forget that I even have the House in Virginia.

(Actually, I always felt uncomfortable around kids, they have that weird soft

spot in their skulls + I have this running phobia that I'll be patting a kid on the head + then my hand will punch through up to my wrist + then I won't be able to get my hand out of the kid's head + then I'll have to explain to the mother why I'm wearing her child's skull like an oven mitt, but, um, I guess that's something entirely different....)

I even have a nice, stable boyfriend with sparkling clean body fluids.

+ after all, it's not like HIV is a death sentence or anything.

Hey, just look at Magic Johnson....

Susan is a stereotypical, Gen X, punk rock, waster writer. Her writing has been accepted by many 'zines that go bankrupt before the first issue. Usually, she is paid for writing in beer + Marlboros. She has spent time in institutions for the mentally...unhealthy.

Bossatrompa Blues
Julien Edmund Moss

Systosomatic
Like myself in another life
I am one soul, one love, one life
I could compose a thousand lines of vomit

I am a schismatic
And I recalled that from a different state
My semipermadrunk mind the more plastic
More pliant than before

Those three jazz ghosts
Mortent aux 60's
And the three Kings
(Pale infidel like me)

The ghosts played of a "free" movement
While the Kings brought of a style from bondage
To elaborate, a kid, a reedsman, and a gestalt
To elucidate, Blues Boy, Southpaw, and Let It Roll

Forget the poetics of Apollo among literary circles
Give yourself instead to the Birdolotry of jazz squares
Holla: For the Bard would have loved the Bird
Lest we forget the copyjobs of dead slingers

Don't forget those who took up
The tenor in recompense to a rhapsode
You was a God, you remember
Your improvisation was supreme

But I'd want to walk with the composers
The Duke to the Monk to the Ming(us)
But somehow I could never just get there
I never had the conception to do that

Julien has been writing since age 3. He has published various illegitimate sketches in the Jibsheet, a weekly newspaper published at Bellevue Community College, where he also graduated in 2007. He's been published in several magazines and blogs including Always Looking, Straylight, Eskimo Pie, Blink Ink, and The Private Acre.

GREED

Sheila Longton

Living above the funeral home that first year, it was me swinging the double doors open at night, flagging the ambulance through, laying the bodies out. Cal was always in the chapel, playing the organ and singing Old Man River and How Great Thou Art in his low, mournful that made everything dreary.

One night, a woman struck by lightning was brought in. I was just drawing the sheet up over her face when her lips moved and she groaned! I screamed, of course, my back pressed to the cold wall, then rushed into the outer room and dialed the director. "If you wouldn't mind stopping by," I said, still shaking, "It's just that I'm not absolutely sure she's dead."

"Sings, too?" The director met me downstairs. "Sounds promising!" He put a mirror to her mouth, held her wrist. "Does it all the time?"

"Only the once. At least that I'm aware of."

He pushed on her chest, a horrible sound like an accordion collapsing.

"There!" I leapt back, my hand at my mouth, "She's alive!"

"Air, passing over the wind pipe is all. Dead the instant the lightning hit. See these fingernails? Smell the burnt flesh? Now. About that singing..."

I realised he meant Cal. "Extra money in it for you if he could do that for services on occasion, set the tone. Might even be a comfort to the family. I'll only take twenty percent."

"I'll let you know," I answered, already dreaming of store-bought socks and a decent sized roasting pan.

"Me? Paid to sing?" Cal was flattered. "But I've no training!" "Think of the families. Such a comfort to them..."

He wanted to do it out of Christian charity.

"You'll do it if it pays, only then." I wanted a new dress, that knick-knack in Woolworth's window, dishes that weren't all cracked and chipped.

Cal sings evenings and weekends. He likes Argyle socks and a turkey every Sunday, hasn't notice the new set. Says he'd like to take singing lessons someday, but I'm saving for that dress.

Sheila Longton is a Canadian. She been published in *Grain, Fiddlehead, Antigonish, The Dalhousie Review, paragraph, Focus on Women, The Times Colonist, Okanagan Sunday Magazine, Homemakers* and *Canadian Living*.

Seven Years With Charlie

Emma Sarappo

DENIAL

It's 4:30.

Charlie will be coming home soon. He'll get off the hulking yellow Norman Pines Elementary school bus and bound towards me with his blue eyes sparkling like diamonds. He'll flash me a million-dollar smile and we'll hold hands as we walk towards the Big House, and I'll ask him, like I always do:

"Hey, Charlie-bear, whatcha got there?"

And he'll say:

"Well, Breena, today I got some work done!" like our daddy taught both of us to say when we were very little, and he'll tell me about his day. Maybe he'll start with how much he loved the cupcake I put into his lunch when Momma wasn't looking, or maybe he'll tell me about Christopher Columbus, or maybe even a book he read, or a fight he was in. I'll listen and I'll smile and I'll tell him about my average high school day, but he'll lose interest and show me a pretty rock or a flower by the side of the driveway. It's okay: I love Charlie's knick knacks much more than I love my day at school.

It's 4:45.

Charlie's not home yet. Sometimes his rickety skeleton of a school bus breaks down. I'll just wait by the stump on the end of the driveway; I wouldn't want him to think that I'm not home. Just a few more minutes, Charlie. I'm here.

I'm still here.

I'm still here…

I don't know what time it is.

I'm sitting by the stump at the end of the winding-snake road that leads up the hill to the Big House, waiting for my little brother. I think the bus already came. I don't see Charlie, though. I'll wait. I'll wait. I'll –

"Breena?"

Momma's home. She's pulled up into the driveway and rolled down her windows, and she's looking at me, headlights glaring at in my eyes. I realize that it's dark out already. What time is it? Where's Charlie?

"Momma?" I ask. I'm a little confused. What's going on?

"Breena, what are you doing?" she asks me in her twanging Alabama accent. She smells like lemongrass perfume, the kind Daddy loves.

"I'm waiting for Charlie," I say dumbly.

Momma starts to tear up. "Breena," she says in a husky voice. "Oh, baby Breena…"

She breaks down on that road, windows down and headlights on, and I can see a thousand moths flying into that source of light expecting comfort, but they're all just dying-every one crushed and burned by the choking engine of our old rusty car.

I see one moth and its wings look like Charlie's hair. I reach out to it, try to convince it not to fly into that headlight, but it does. I see in my mind's eye Charlie, laughing and playing with Daddy, and then I see him drop the ball. It rolls into the road while I'm sketching in the crunchy Alabama grass and Charlie goes after it. I see the car turn the bend on the road and I scream, but it's too late…

I see the blood- oh, Lord, there's so much blood!

Then I see a frenzy of people and white coats and white linens in a white hospital, and finally I see Charlie on a slab with white skin and I scream. I choke on my own horror, and then I scream again, and I'm back in the present and I'm still screaming and my eyes sting- and my knees buckle, and I can't breathe, and I grab for my momma,

I break down with Momma on our winding country driveway in the warm August night, the kinds that smell like bonfires and insect repellent. I reach through the window to hold her. We cry.

ANGER

I'm in my room.

I'm on my bed.

I want to scream.

I want someone to pay.

Charlie was the best kid alive, you know. He had feather-down hair and the deepest blue eyes you've ever seen, like wells of love. Charlie loved everything- he loved our family, he loved our house, he loved his friends- and his enemies, too. Mostly, though, he really loved fireflies. His heart pumped ambrosia love instead of blood.

"They're little lights showing the way to God," Daddy used to say to him. "They're not an actual path to Heaven, Charlie, just little miracles to remind us how great creation really is."

He would catch them all in a jar and let their light shine for a few minutes, and then he would open the jar and laugh as they all flew away in little spirals of light. I loved how Charlie loved it.

I remember when he was born. Momma brought him home from the hospital, wrapped up as perfect as an angel from God, and Daddy took us out in the field- me, Momma, Daddy, and little baby Charlie- and we sat in the grass and looked up at the sky.

"Breena," said Daddy, "this is a big step for our family. We've been blessed with a little boy and his name is Charlie, and he needs a lot of attention and a lot of patience. Mostly, though, he needs you. You're his big sister, Breena. You have to promise to love him and help him out when he needs it. You gotta give him advice when he wants it and even when he doesn't. You gotta look out for him, you hear?"

"Yes, sir," I said solemnly.

"Well, then, Breena," he said in his raspy southern smoker voice, conjuring up images of the dark, humid, Vietnam jungle, Daddy's cigarette lighting up like a firefly with his unit members around him, "here you go. This is yours officially." He handed me a leather bracelet with his leathery hands, calloused and worn, but full of warmth, and I put it on. It said "SISTER"- corny, shoddily engraved, made with without skill, but leaking love, and that's when I became his sister- not before, not when he was born- when I promised to love him. I grew up that day.

I'm still on my bed.

The sheets are tangled in me. I am tangled in the sheets. They're knots around my hands and knees and as much as I'd like to get up and destroy something- the house, the property, the whole state of Alabama- I can't. I'm caught in the net.

I'm still wearing the bracelet. I feel it on my wrist and the rough leather touch of it brings me to a rough, roaring rage. All this anger is bottlenecked inside of me, and my cap is about to burst off like a firework. I can see myself, filling with rage, everything inside of me melting from sheer rage until I am nothing but a rolling tide of blood, burning the house, burning the road, burning the world.

I imagine Charlie's laugh, and the cap bursts. I scream.

"WHY HIM?" I yell. I'm rolling around, I'm sobbing- I look a mess. This spectacle is a mess. "COME ON, GOD, CHARLIE? WHY CHARLIE...?" The rest trails off into a crescendo of a scream, which becomes sobs, which becomes hiccups, which trails into nothing. I am nothing but anger.

I don't go to church that Sunday. How can I worship God if He took Charlie from me?

BARGAINING

"I'm sorry," I begin my prayer at night. "Dear Lord, I'm sorry I didn't go to church on Sunday. I was angry. Lord, please watch over this family and this house and please give your grace to the world. Amen."

I pull the covers over my head and roll over. I close my eyes. I try to sleep.

Fast forward five minutes later- I'm up again. "Dear Lord. I will be a better person. I will give all my clothes to Goodwill. I will do anything. I will do anything, Lord, if you just let me... if you let me talk to Charlie."

I squeeze my hands and my eyes together real tight and hold my breath. I wait. A minute passes and I don't hear Charlie's laugh, but I roll over with a sigh. Maybe God is busy. He has a lot of stuff to do, you know.

When Charlie was five, I turned sixteen. I loved him so much, but I was sixteen and the social hierarchy of high school flourished. I was so excited- my 'cool' friends were coming over for my party, and I couldn't let them see him! He was five, immature, had a habit for saying nasty words he learned from Daddy (who really, really hated when the Cowboys lost) and followed me around to such an extent I had to leave the bathroom door open for him, so I sat down and I pleaded with him.

"Charlie-bear," I started. "Listen here. I'm turning sixteen now, and-"

"Six... ten!" he cried, holding up six, then all ten fingers. I felt a rush of guilt.

"Yeah, that's right," I said, shushing him, "but the thing is, Charlie, I'm getting big. I'm way bigger than five. See, it's gonna be big girls hanging out at this party, and I just think you should work on... um, try perfecting your Lego castle! Then you can show it to me and-"

Any other five year old would have happily agreed, but Charlie was smart, he knew what I was up to. "Why can't I come to your party, Breena?" he asked, lower lip trembling.

"Charlie, no, that's not... That's not what I meant," I cried.

Charlie was already crying, and I looked down at my bracelet- SISTER. I had a Saturday TV special kind of revelation, the kind with a moral and a Bible passage, but it was sincere. I wasn't being a good big sister.

"Hey, buddy," I said, kneeling down. "I'm sorry. I want you at my party. You can blow my candles out," I said, and I gave him a huge hug.

"I love you, Breena," he whispered.

They say turning sixteen is a milestone. I say my little brother was a milestone on his own.

I just woke up from my memories. I figure another try can't hurt.

"I swear, Lord, I swear that if you let me talk to Charlie I will do anything at all. Anything, anything. Please."

Again, I am silent.

Again, there is no reply.

DEPRESSION

My room is a prison.

I don't get out of bed any more. I hardly eat, and I sleep all of the time.

I miss Charlie.

I know intimately everything in this room. I know the powdery paper-thin plaster walls, ready to fold like a house of cards. I know the desk in the corner, full of papers that are meaningless leaves on a useless tree. I know every broken, sagging spring in my mattress that I flop so often upon. I know every crevice in my bedframe. I know where it's chipped because Charlie threw a baseball at it.

I know the ceiling. I know every drip of plaster in every confounding pattern or guilt and sadness mapped across the roof.

I wish I didn't know anything.

I ask at least once daily. "Why Charlie?"

I think at least twice: "Why live?"

My Grandmama was a tiger packed into a five foot old woman. She was the smartest person I ever knew, not just with school, but with life. Her eyes were two wise little marbles set into a curtain of draping skin, and she always had advice whenever I needed it. She lived with us, but she really lived on her rocking chair by the Big House, knitting or watching the critters run through the grass. She died before Charlie was born, and when she did, I was lost.

Grandmama was cremated, her ashes spread over this Alabama country home. Daddy sat down with me on our land and held me while I cried. I remember his dirt-stained overalls and his cigarette, and how the smoke from it danced around in the wind. He looked at me with his serious eyes.

"Breena," he said, "do you smell that?"

"No," I sniffed. "I don't smell anything."

"No, honey, you just don't notice it. Take a great big whiff. That's the smell of Alabama summertime- that's the smell of our sweat and our tears and our hard work and our home. Now- smell again. That's the scent of your Grandmama. Whenever you miss her, you gotta remember that she's always there with you- all you gotta do is smell the air."

We were quiet for a moment.

"You're growing up, Breena," said Daddy. "You're becoming a fine young lady. But you have responsibilities. You have to take what Grandmama gave you, all of her wisdom and what she taught you, and you have to use it, you hear me? You can't spend your time missing her. You have to keep on living."

I nodded and smelled the air.

Charlie was buried in the Norman Pines cemetery in a cedar box, but I can still smell him in everything in this home. I smell his hair and I smell his laughter and I smell cedar, but it's all him.

ACCEPTANCE

My little brother, Charlie John Wincrest, died when he was hit by a car. He was seven years old. I miss him every second of every minute of every day, and sometimes it hits me so hard I can't breathe, but I've realized that he's dead. He's not coming back. Life is for the living and I'm making Charlie a promise to treasure the firefly in every moment of every Alabama summer, and I will always remember the stump at the end of the driveway. I'll never stop laughing at that rickety old school bus, and I'll always treasure our memories. Looking back, I realize Charlie's life was the catalyst to me growing up. I learned to smell the Alabama air, I became a big sister, and I turned sixteen. I'm not the same person I was- and I suppose it was all a rite of passage designed by some higher power much wiser than I am. Charlie being alive was important to me, and to my family, and to everyone he met, but it was also important to him. Charlie Wincrest grew up to be a loving little boy, and finally he went through the last rite of passage that we all must face: death. The loss of such a young kid is always a tragedy, especially in a small town like Norman Pines, but it was no accident. We were given Charlie for a reason, and we lost him for a reason, but it was him who made me who I am, and I thank him.

I've accepted it. I've grown up. I console myself with the thought that Charlie finally got to meet his Grandmama, and in the Alabama summertime, I always try to catch fireflies.

Emma Sarappo is an honors student at Sunset Middle School. Born in Pasadena, CA but raised outside of Nashville TN, Emma's hobbies include reading and drawing. She has been riding horses for many years and likes to spend time with her cats. Emma will graduate in 2015 from Ravenwood High School in Brentwood, TN. College aspirations lean toward Pre-Law or Engineering.

Lonely Hearts

Charles Greaves

LONELY HEARTS #241
21 YO SBF, pretty face, nice smile,
curvaceous body.
NS social drinker.
Enjoy film and live music.
Hoping to meet a friend first
and see what develops.

      I should have gotten up and walked out. I should have said something.
What I did, though, was lift the fork to my mouth and took a bite of the over-
salted pot roast, because that's what fat girls do.

      My name is Alicia Gardener, Class of 1979 - William Tollman High
School, and I wrote that ad.   It cost seventeen dollars and fifty cents of my own
money to see it in four editions of the weekly *Pawtucket Standard*. My hope was
to mitigate the first impression my "curves" might make on a date, and instead
impress someone with my personality.

      My Dad's name is Al Gardener, not Albert, just Al. My brother and I
lived with Dad and his new girlfriend, while Mom lived out of state. They
decided my brother and I would be better off finishing school here in Pawtucket.
Mom moved to Florida after they divorced. The new girlfriend was an older,
dyed blond white woman that my Dad most likely had been sleeping with long

before he divorced, but we never discussed it. My brother and I didn't discuss much anymore either, in a way it was like being a boarder in a dysfunctional bed and breakfast. I could have moved out, I was 19 now, but I wanted to graduate Junior College first. In truth, I was afraid; afraid to be alone, afraid to fail, afraid I would never find someone to hold my hand or talk to me. Class of '79 and never been kissed.

Dad was adamant about us eating at the big dining table every night, as though everything was normal still. When my Mom first left, my brother and I would do the shopping and cook as best we could. It made us feel, in some small way, like a family. Dad seemed appreciative of our efforts, until "She" moved in. When the new girlfriend came along, we were driven from the kitchen. She quickly let us know that cooking was not our job anymore. My brother tried to compensate by cleaning up, but nothing he did was ever good enough. He either stacked the plates in the wrong place, or he used the wrong container for leftovers; so he stopped trying, we both stopped trying.

I had waited weeks for a reply to my ad.   Lonely Hearts replies went to a central blind ad address, then the letter would be forwarded, unopened, to the ad's owner.   This would insure the anonymity of whoever placed the ad. I should say it was supposed to.

Outside the window, I could see the lilacs blooming, and school would be over for the semester in a few weeks. From my father's fingers dangled a thick blue envelope. He opened the envelope and removed a single sheet of lined note paper. "This came in the mail today; I don't think it's for me, though," he said, as he pushed the little half glasses up on his nose. Dad smiled and began to read aloud,

Hi,

    My name is Eric. I'm 25 years old.

    I am quite tall; hope you like tall guys. I have steady work with my Uncle and have my own car. Sometimes I go to hear live music, or to see a movie. Do you like tall guys?

    I like that you're a curvy woman. I like that. My arms are long and strong, so I could easily hug you.

    I have included my phone number. I live with my Mom; she might answer, but you can just ask for me.

    I hope you will call.

    We can meet someplace for coffee and talk.

                     -   Eric Besser

Dad folded the letter slowly and smiled. "Big long arms, sounds like that boy could swing from a tree."

I took another bite, swallowed hard, and washed it down with iced tea. The new girlfriend smiled through her painted lips. My brother looked as though he was trying to disappear.

Dad took the envelope and finally handed it to me. "So you placed an ad in the paper, an ad for a boy?" he asked.

"Hush, Al. Lots of people place ads, they are called Lonely Hearts ads, right dear?" said the painted lips. She made a little flutter with her fingers. A dismissive gesture.

I glanced at the envelope. On the upper left corner it said Lonely Hearts. It was addressed:

A. Gardener
40 Shoal Rd.
Pawtucket, R.I.

Could my Dad have honestly thought it was addressed to him? If so, might he have read it to himself and then handed it to me discreetly?   An embarrassed father-daughter moment might ensue. Instead he reads it aloud at the table with her there. Why? Was my pathetic attempt to find a date a joke to be shared? Did he think there was some life lesson for me to learn from this; some parental tradition to toughen the thin skin of a naive child?

That envelope sat by my glass of iced tea while we finished dinner. I didn't let my gaze drift anywhere near it. My Dad made small talk as though nothing horrible had just happened. When I had eaten enough to be excused, more than enough, I took the envelope to my room and opened it. I couldn't read it. I wouldn't read it. I wasn't even sure I would ever call Mr. Eric Besser.

What I did was take the latest copy of <u>Modern Romance and Mystery</u> from under my pillow and an open box of Malamars that lay on my nightstand. Next I cried. I took a bite and let the Malamars' chocolate coating melt in my mouth, wishing I could disappear into the story. That's what fat girls do.

Charles had his story, "The Light Fantastic", recently published in the 2010 Writers' Circle Anthology. He's recently recorded a collection of original children's stories and music titled, "Good Stories for Great Kids", working with producer Tucker Dalton. Charles lives in an old barn with a good guitar and a comfortable chair and is finishing up his first novel.

The Land Of 10

Martino Hooghkirk

What is in the land of ten,
A little closer to all the men.
Almost no more babying from mom,
It will be a bit more calm.

Now only if I were really eleven,
That would certainly be heaven.
Then I could stay up a lot later,
That would be so much greater.

Then what if I were actually thirteen,
I'd be finally part of the scene.
I would have a lot more friends,
To help me work 'round the bends.

Now sixteen wouldn't be too bad,
Because I'll have stuff I never had.
I could drive a car and get a job,
And not sit around like a lazy blob.

Then best of all is thirty-six,
Making my dinners from dinner mix.
A house, a job, a dirty pool,
Wait! That doesn't sound too cool.

What's wrong with nine?
It's quite divine.
No rules or bills or work all day,
Just left with time for fun and play!

I guess I'll stick with my age nine,
It is actually quite fine.
I see I've got nothing to fear,
But I still can't wait until next year!

Martino is a 7th grader with a great passion for words. He is an avid reader who also loves to write. He lives in Franklin, TN with his parents and three siblings. His interest in words expand beyond English, in fact he is bilingual and fluent both in English and Italian, since his mother is Italian and his father American.

THE
DEER
PARK

KEVIN P.
KEATING

I

An abrupt rush of cold air whistles through the front window of the cab, wrenching Edward de Vere from his gloomy ruminations. The driver, wreathed in silver smoke, clamps the smoldering butt of a cigarette between his tragic stumps of teeth and makes another small adjustment to the rearview mirror.

"You do not mind?"

De Vere shakes his head. No, the smoke doesn't bother him, not terribly. After the violent confrontation that morning with his thieving son and the subsequent argument with his wife about the family's financial troubles, de Vere discovers that he has become almost completely numb to pain, to pleasure, to the unvarying drone of his own thoughts.

From the pocket of his camelhair coat, he retrieves the flask inscribed with his initials (a gift from an utterly forgettable mistress), and with a wistful smile, takes a healthy swig of absinthe. De Vere has come to rely on the stuff. The effects are strictly spiritual of course, not particularly good for his ulcer or for his reasoning faculties, enemies of the mystical experience, but somehow it makes these evenings a little more interesting, less predictable. The liquor sears his esophagus, ignites the walls of his gut, spreads like a vast oil plume across the surface of his consciousness, illuminating the murkiest depths of his soul with tongues of Pentecostal fire. He relishes the sensation.

"Where are you going tonight, sir?" asks the driver.

"Oh, nowhere in particular."

Because he doesn't want to sound like just another slurring drunk in the back of a cab during the midnight hours, de Vere lifts his chin, purses his lips, and attempts to enunciate each syllable, each hard consonant, and nasally vowel, but he stumbles over that last word--<u>par-tic-u-lar</u>--and realizes, with some chagrin, that he can no longer disguise his old accent, can't soften the working class cadences that for so many years marked him as a poseur. Lost is the patrician affectation he has fine-tuned since his days as a student at the Jesuit school. The ruse is finally up: his words lack authority; they carry no more weight than if spoken by any predacious degenerate born and raised in this blighted section of town.

Deciding it best to keep his mouth shut, he uses simple hand gestures to direct the driver deeper into the city's most destitute and ungovernable quarters, an anxious journey without compass or charts. De Vere probes every garbage-strewn corner, every shuttered window, every dangerous alley. Things are desolate now, but it's only a matter of time before the crazies, decked out in wild costumes, emerge from their shanties and squalid apartment blocks to celebrate under the power lines and behind the chain-linked fences crowned with barbed wire. It's Halloween, a night sacred to the unhinged mind, but de Vere now sees a deeper pattern and believes it doesn't matter what day or hour it happens to be. They are everywhere, these lunatics, a never-ending parade of human ruin, a plague cast down from heaven in a way that hints at God's indifference to the world.

"It is unusually quiet this evening," says the driver, his eyes nervously scanning the streets.

De Vere tries to suppress a knowing smile. Soon this little preserve will be positively teeming with game, and the idea--of a hunter and his quarry--makes him wonder if in a former life he had been a gentleman of quality who frequented the private hunting grounds of the king, invited by His Majesty to a country chateau to spend holidays shooting impressive white-tailed stags and, at day's end, violating young wenches behind a stand of blue pines.

De Vere's wife is convinced that he is an old soul, that he has undergone innumerable incarnations as insect, beast, vassal, and lord. "You're afflicted with the curse of metempsychosis," she explained to him one night.

He sighs and fingers through the dwindling cash in his money clip. If only she could gaze into her crystal ball and divine a simple solution to their financial difficulties--maybe he would be in Paris, Copenhagen, Amsterdam instead of marooned in the city of his birth, riding in the back of a yellow cab that rumbles like a tank in the final cataclysmic scene of some generic wartime melodrama, the rusted muffler scraping along the ridges and fissures in the road, the brakes screeching and grinding at every turn, the radio hissing and crackling and occasionally exploding with unintelligible outbursts from an angry dispatcher. Suddenly de Vere feels not like an aristocrat waited on by a liveried footman but a magician's assistant stuffed into a tiny black box, waiting to be impaled by sharp objects.

From the rearview mirror dark eyes study him. They blink in rapid succession as if trying to untangle his snarled storyline, the profusion of lives he has lived.

"Family troubles?"

De Vere lowers his flask. "Why do you ask?"

"I have been driving this cab for many years now, yes, many years. Women, children, they take their toll on a man. I have come to recognize the symptoms."

"Perhaps you can describe these…symptoms."

The driver chuckles and expertly flicks his cigarette out the window. "Well, for one, you have a certain look of resignation. Also, a look of distrust in your eyes. But of course a man can never trust the people he loves. No, not entirely."

De Vere crosses his arms, shifts uneasily in the backseat. "I don't trust anyone. My son is a thief, my best friend is a gullible fool, and I'm starting to think my wife is a borderline sociopath trying to poison me. She's developed a fascination for alternative medicine. Witchcraft." He shrugs his shoulders. "It's a cliché, I know, but only my dog remains loyal to me."

He feels some shame for divulging the details of his life to a complete stranger, but like a lot of people he knows, too many really, de Vere has become more and more involved in his own problems; he cultivates them, multiplies them, makes them deeper and richer than if he left them alone to spin round and round his brain.

The driver nods. "Why do we trouble ourselves over such things, eh? Wives, sons, they are of little consequence. Life is merely something to endure. Like a disease. Repose will come soon enough."

De Vere smirks. "Repose? Yes. Or absolution. I would settle for that."

"You are a man with deep religious convictions?"

De Vere considers this for a moment, notices the small statue of Saint Fiacre on the dashboard. "I thought about becoming an atheist, but then I realized atheism requires more devotion."

The driver laughs, a low gritty sound like the crunch and grind of asphalt beneath the tires. "Indeed," he says, "an atheist must be diligent. There is always the temptation to believe in a fearsome god or in a tempting devil. And any nightmarish circumstance can quickly cure a man of his apostasy."

De Vere isn't interested in advice, if that is what this meddlesome man is offering. No one can convince him that what he is doing is wrong, certainly not the cabdriver who will soon discover the truth for himself; not the abstinence-stricken priests who listen to de Vere's expurgated confessions on Saturday afternoons and wait for the appropriate moment to beg him for more filthy lucre; not his wife who suspects him of every kind of misdeed and then attempts to exorcize the demons of infidelity by encouraging him to ingest a hundred different homeopathic potions that are as evil-smelling as they are toxic; not even his perpetually dour best friend to whom he confides every wretched detail late at night in the disquieting calm of his study.

There are too many moral crusaders in the world, each with an equally improbable scheme to lead a man to salvation, a million cures for a million vices--through prayer, repentance, self-flagellation--but when he looks through the portal that separates reality from the hereafter, de Vere sees not the treasures of heaven but the fiery pools of hell. Having already dipped his toes in the scalding waters, he wonders if he can finally muster the courage to submerge himself

fully in what the Jesuits warn is "total depravity." Of course, most people have no way of knowing just how sublime the river of sin can be, how thrilling to be swept away and carried off to a place you never intended to go. Or maybe they do. The world, as de Vere knows from experience, is full of irredeemable hypocrites.

II

Six months ago, when he first embarked on these forbidden excursions, de Vere preferred to use his own car, but then late one evening, while idling at a red light, a group of teenage boys, oozing with adolescent virulence, materialized from the shadows. They made lewd gestures, rapped on his door, spat on his windshield. Phlegm hung in heavy green beads from the tinted glass. An intolerable situation. He wasn't about to let this gang of little brown bastards fuck with his lady. No, that would never do. Aside from an occasional trip to the slums, de Vere's ostentatious European touring car may be the only thing that offers him some satisfaction in this world. He read somewhere that cars are modeled on the female form, and there is, he finds, something rather arousing about its sleek and elegant design, the exaggerated curves of the rear end, the heady scent of leather, the breathless moans of the V6 engine. With mounting agitation, he put his hand on the door handle, fully prepared to kick some ass, but from the corner of his eye he caught the flash of a knife blade. De Vere hit the gas hard and thundered away. Gloating with triumph, he opened the sunroof and raised his middle finger. From this incident he has learned two invaluable lessons: victory always belongs to the man with the most torque and horsepower, and more importantly, it's best to take a taxi to and from the hunting grounds.

Of course these monthly outings wouldn't be necessary if he hadn't mismanaged the melancholy business of his marriage. He has grown indifferent toward his wife. Over the years she has become irreparably tarnished, another neglected objet d'art in his immense and uncatalogued collection of conquests. Sex with her is boring, pedestrian, another tedious obligation like walking the dog or attending mass on Sunday morning. He thought about ending things once and for all, getting his lawyers involved, but a messy divorce right now would only hasten his destruction. He is already on the brink of financial collapse. Until the economy picks up, he must bide his time, explore other avenues.

To his surprise he finds that company parties and gala dinners aren't exactly conducive to casual encounters with members of the opposite sex, especially when the tiny breasted ladies, with their taut puritanical faces and severe prudish frowns, waste so much time droning on and on about disgustingly conventional subjects: their learning disabled children, their lazy and inadequate husbands, their terminally ill parents, their insipid duties as accountants and business analysts. He manages to seduce a college intern or two, but even they insist on old-fashioned gentleness and solicitude, and he quickly learns that a comfortable lifestyle doesn't necessarily entitle a man to possess a secret harem of pretty girls (or even a few plain ones for that matter). Though he wants no entanglements, he has an acute understanding of the rules of the game and, for a little while at least, he abides by them, purchases a few extravagant gifts, vials of perfume, diamond tennis bracelets, spa treatments, reservations for wine and cheese tastings, and in exchange for these creature comforts, he expects his mistresses to submit to his modest desires and then to vanish once he tires of their shrill voices.

But things never work out this way, certainly not in suburbia where all eroticism is crushed to a fine powder and scattered in the wind like ashes from a funeral pyre, the burnt offerings of impetuous youth, and any lingering impetuosity in a man de Vere's age is regarded as perversion, plain and simple. Unusual delights, if they are to be found at all, must come from these midnight hunts through the streets of a post-industrial wasteland. This haunt of sweet sin does not discriminate: here every man is welcome, and sex remains a constant fount of miracles. Although he is somewhat familiar with the terrain and can still recall the forsaken avenues and narrow brick lanes from his days at the Jesuit high school, he is keenly aware of the dangers all around.

III

After circling a particularly dismal block for the third time--three, that charming number--de Vere glimpses a pack of stray dogs trotting through the tempered light, wretched curs bred in brutal haste in slimy culverts and under the skeleton tracks of a rotting train trestle. In their tireless quest for food, they topple a trashcan outside an apartment building, the vaguely familiar Zanzibar Towers & Gardens, and fight over a hunk of putrid meat, a sheet of greasy wax paper smeared with red juices, a container of cookies, a headless doll. Snarling their disapproval, the brindled mongrels watch the cab roll by. De Vere feels a close connection to these animals, admires the purity of their instincts. Nature has conferred upon them some special power for reading the minds of men. He wonders if they can sniff out the stench of desperation that drips from his pores and clings to his shirt, his cashmere sweater, his indispensable silk boxers.

"Mongrels…" the driver mutters, swerving to avoid the beer cans that clatter into the street.

Something catches de Vere's eye. With a tantalizing mixture of eagerness and dread, he sits up, adjusts his collar and sleeves, glides a practiced finger across his professionally whitened teeth. "Stop the cab," he orders.

"But, sir, there are troublemakers about."

"I said stop the cab!"

"Very well."

De Vere rolls down the window, clears his throat, and boldly addresses the woman who has just emerged from the apartment building. "Excuse me, miss!"

Through the partition, the driver whispers, "Sir, she is chattel, a loathsome thing. Vile."

"Miss, a moment of your time."

"I beg of you, sir, I cannot possibly…"

With an almost regal bearing, the woman struts across the street in a pair of incredible red boots. A pickup swerves to avoid her. In the bed of the truck several young men shout with malice. "Puta! Mujerzuela! Almeja!" Spellbound, de Vere watches her and wonders what has gone wrong in her life, why she doesn't work in an office building like the rest of the women he knows; it takes next to nothing to sit in a cubicle and pretend to be busy for most of the day. In the business world, one's appearance means everything, and she can't very well show up to an important meeting dressed in a purple miniskirt, her cheeks smeared with rouge, her eyes ringed with mascara like warm, wet ash.

"Hey, sweet thing," she says, leaning against the cab. "You lookin' for some company?"

"As a matter of fact…" Feeling almost amorous, he offers the woman his flask.

"Oh, that's some good shit, baby," she rasps after taking a sip.

"Remarkable," says de Vere, stroking the woman's hand. "A woman who appreciates the green-eyed monster. I think I'm in love."

She suppresses a belch. "Green-eyed, one-eyed, it's all the same to me."

"Marvelous! What's your name, darling?"

"Name's Tamar, baby."

"How unusual. You're not busy this evening, are you, Tamar?"

"Just finished working a big soiree. Right up there." She points to a window crowded with silhouettes at the Zanzibar Towers & Gardens. "But I'm free now. Well, maybe not free."

De Vere opens the door and moves over so the woman can slide in beside him.

The driver hisses. "Sir, I will not be a party to this kind of thing."

De Vere clicks his tongue. By now his response has become automatic, a maddeningly predictable exchange between master and servant. He passes the customary amount of money through the partition and watches the driver count the bills one at a time. It always surprises him how readily these men of conscience transform themselves into purveyors of pleasure, how willing they are to implicate themselves in his crimes and to share in his guilt.

"Very well then," says the driver. "But one day, sir, one day soon, when she can no longer serve her purpose, this woman will be discovered in an alley with her throat slashed. No questions will be asked. No investigation will be conducted. Among these people, life is a brief visitor. It's just as well. More time on this earth would bring little in the way of happiness to such a creature."

As the cab rolls away from the curb, de Vere becomes aware of the driver watching him in the rearview mirror. He has gotten used to this, too. They always watch, these drivers; they are depraved, the whole damned world is depraved, and so he decides to give the man a show, the standard pornography. He unzips his pants, bunches the woman's black hair in his fists and forces her into a syncopated rhythm. She stinks to high heaven, reeks of chemicals, lighter fluid, formaldehyde, an odor he can't quite place. She probably hasn't bathed in days. This in itself doesn't bother him. In fact, there is something erotic about her filthiness. It makes his knees tremble. Besides, he always comes prepared to deal with unpleasant details. From his coat pocket he produces a bottle of eau de toilette and spritzes the back of her neck.

She lifts her head. "The fuck you doin'?"

"Shut up and keep going."

"Why you gotta talk that way?"

"Finish the goddamn job."

The woman resumes bobbing up and down in de Vere's lap, her movements so wild, so relentless, so crazed, that he is afraid she might tear into him with her chipped teeth. He groans, rocks his hips back and forth. Then he feels the taxi shudder violently and almost stall.

He opens his eyes, knocks on the partition. "What the hell is it now? Why are you slowing down?"

"I think they're following us," the driver tells him. "Yes, there is no doubt about it. They are definitely following us."

"What are you talking about?"

"You see, this is what they do. Like hunters they lurk in the shadows and then trounce on their prey. Ruthless."

"Who?"

"The police."

De Vere turns his head, sees a cruiser riding the back bumper. "Dammit, your taillight is out."

"Nonsense."

"I noticed it when I climbed inside this fucking tin can."

The driver scowls. "They obviously spotted you luring that slut into my cab. I cannot afford to go to jail again. Please, ask her to stop."

But de Vere can't do that, not now, not even as the cruiser pursues them through the absurd serpentine streets, not even when the siren starts its terrible piercing wail, and the blue and white lights blind him. He digs his nails into the seat and lets out a rapturous cry: "Oh, God! Maybe this is my road to Damascus!"

The driver hits the breaks and puts the cab in park. "Drunken fool, keep your mouth shut. Or I promise…things will not go well for you."

An officer approaches the cab, hitches his belt, but instead of interrogating the driver, he opens the back door, grabs the woman by the wrist and drags her over to the sidewalk. She wipes her chin with the back of her hand and pulls the hem of her skirt down so her panties don't show.

"Still turning tricks, eh, Tamar? Funny. Thought we told you we didn't want to see you around here anymore. Didn't we tell you that? You gonna answer me? I know you ain't deaf, Tamar. Stupid yes, deaf no."

A German shepherd bounds toward the cab, its teeth barred, a long rope of saliva swinging in a wide arc from its snapping jaws. Another patrol car arrives. Radio scanners screech and croak and erupt with high, thin whistles. The officer turns his flashlight on de Vere, who is so overcome with dread that he can only sit there like a bewildered toddler, pants around his ankles, a look of drooling incomprehension on his face.

"Whatcha doing in this neighborhood, pal? You like coming to this part of town? You a regular?" Impatient with de Vere's infantile sputtering, the officer yanks him from the cab and pushes him against the trunk. "Christ almighty, pull up your pants, you animal! Now, put your hands behind your back." He slaps on the cuffs, reaches into de Vere's camelhair coat, confiscates his flask, his wallet, the bottle of perfume.

"Wait a minute," says de Vere, "this isn't the road to Damascus…"

"Damascus? No, buddy, we're taking you downtown."

"You're making a grave mistake. I know people, important people. They'll tell you. I'm a reputable businessman, a loving husband and father."

De Vere's voice is shrill, manic. He struggles, thrashes his legs, but the officer slings an arm around his neck and squeezes tight until de Vere begins to gasp for air.

"Just cooperate, okay, bud? You don't want an assault charge tacked on, do ya?"

As chapel bells begin to chime the witching hour, a raucous crowd spills from the gaping double doors of the Zanzibar Towers & Gardens. Apparently the cab has been going in circles, and now de Vere must endure the laughter of priests and pregnant nuns and a bloated Lazarus wrapped in rags. They drink and smoke and dance, some of them grinding violently against each other, feigning copulation. On the sidewalk a man whirls round and round, his dreadlocks rising above his head like the tentacles of some fabled sea creature. Last to emerge from the building is a tall figure in the blood red robes of a grand inquisitor, a sagacious and unreasonably cruel arbiter of the laws of God and man. With a subtle flick of his wrist he silences the discordant howls and jeers of his grotesque entourage.

De Vere lurches heavily, falls to his knees, and humbly pleads his case before his fellow darkness worshippers. "Listen to me. Would you please listen? Tomorrow morning I'll go straight to the chapel. I'll light a candle before a statue of the Virgin. I'll make a vow before the Lord to live a life of celibacy..."

His head starts to spin. The absinthe percolates in the pit of his stomach and suddenly surges up his throat, a hot green sludge that splatters the officer's polished black shoes and the cuffs of his pants.

"Motherfucker!"

The other cops laugh. "Hey, Caddigan, have fun cleaning that shit."

"Fuck you. I ain't touching it."

De Vere gasps and sputters, "I'm sorry, so sorry..."

Then he feels a sharp crack against his spine, a quick spasm of pain that shoots down to the tips of his toes, and things go dark for a little while.

IV

Mumbling piteous oaths, fighting against the cuffs that dig into his wrists, de Vere drifts in and out of consciousness, and for one incredible moment, he feels himself turn to vapor and slip through a small crack at the top of the back window. With a covey of fractious grackles, he flies high above the church spires and spins around the gothic tower of the Jesuit school. Out over the lake a storm rages, and the gathering clouds drape him in the bruised colors of high-autumn--cadmium reds and yellows. A strong gust of wind transports him over the great steel bridge that spans the crooked river and hurtles him along the city streets. He slides down a sparkling glass atrium and lands in a bustling emporium of fashionable restaurants and nightclubs where stunted boys, wearing sandwich boards, blunder among a group of portly men in pinstriped suits and emaciated women in skimpy cocktail dresses.

De Vere's eyes flutter open. He is pulled from the back of the police cruiser, lifted to his feet, and dragged into headquarters. At the front desk he is made to stand at attention. "Another dirty married man," someone quips. Boiling white light seeps behind his eye sockets and scalds his brain. He waits there for hours, it seems, but eventually, mercifully, he is booked for indecent exposure, public intoxication, solicitation of prostitution, a long recitation of trumped-up charges. He hears the words, but they do not make any sense to him, and at this point he doesn't really care what they mean. He is photographed, fingerprinted, his body searched for contraband. Manacled and moaning like an idiot that lurches from some horror movie dungeon, he is led through a series of endless corridors that echo with tortured screams, like someone being stabbed over and over with a penknife.

An alarm sounds. A clanking steel door rolls open, and he is shoved into a large holding cell swarming with flies. He collapses beside a mysterious yellow stream that trickles toward a drain. After a few minutes he becomes dimly aware that he is not alone. Other men, dozens of them, each indistinguishable from the other, materialize like shades from the underworld. All suffer the afflictions and burdens of anonymity, their faces transformed into primitive masks, wooden idols with wooden scowls.

The men close in, their eyes unwavering. Unlike the police they do not ask him to cooperate. They taunt him, playfully at first as children sometimes do with a puppy or a kitten to see how it will react, and once they determine he is harmless, they begin to slap him in earnest, jab him in the kidneys, stomp on his fingers, yank him by the hair. He doesn't struggle for long. They force him to his knees, tell him to open wide, not to bite.

"Gonna get me some slop on my knob."

"Mmmm, yeah, get my salad tossed, that's what I'm talkin' 'bout."

"You like that, don't you, bitch?"

"Do a good job now, or they gonna carry your ass out in a body bag."

With this warning, they line up ten deep, some massaging themselves in preparation, spirits of the dead eager to douse him in ectoplasm. He lifts his head and recognizes the small, feral eyes of the man standing at the front of the line.

"Good evening, my friend," says the cabdriver. "Life, as you know, consists of little more than the ebb and flow of excessive pleasure and pain, wave upon wave of joy and sorrow. Unfortunately, you have found yourself in a deep trough. But do not fear. It will not always be so for you. Fate is ever changing. Oblivion alone is imperishable."

Then the driver unbuckles his belt and, with a smile that reveals those unsightly gray stumps, whispers, "And now, if you please, there are many men waiting…"

KEVIN P. KEATING'S essays and fiction have appeared in a number of literary journals, including Slow Trains, Green Hills Literary Lantern, Subtle Tea, Cerebration, Fiction Warehouse, The Plum Ruby Review, Ascent Aspirations, Double Dare Press, Tattoo Highway and many others. His short story "The Black Death of Gentile da Foligno" (Perigee, 2007) was nominated for a Pushcart Prize by Thomas E. Kennedy. His novel, The Natural Order of Things, is scheduled for publication in mid-2011 by Northern Frights Publishing. He currently teaches English at Baldwin-Wallace College near Cleveland, Ohio.

Stanley B. Trice — Peter Sleeps

Peter resisted sleep for as long as he could by calling her name and remembering her blue eyes. But, it was how he killed his wife Ann that really kept him awake.

Peter took a chance she would not die where he killed her. He thought her the stronger and able to resist the urge to give up on life. At least until he got her to the hospital and he could be made the hero instead of a murderer. But, he was wrong. Ann was finished with this life and being killed by Peter satisfied her. Peter might have realized this if had not been too caught up trying to kill himself.

Peter thought that maybe Ann didn't understand his selfishness and tried to stop him. No, they had been married for forty two years and it had worn on them. She wanted to die first. Too late, Peter decided they were in competition. He should have known this after their last argument when Ann told him she wanted to be dead.

"You're the reason we don't have children. You're infertile," she said.

"You're the reason we don't have friends. You're depressing," Peter said.

"In all these years, you are all I'm left with," Ann said. A glimmer of hate spoke in her blue eyes.

"I have nothing to say to you after all these years," Peter said. "This is all we have."

That was how it would be with them, Peter decided. Of course, this left only one way out for him. Except, Ann thought this, too. He did not think she was that courageous.

As he held her face tight in his hands, Peter wondered if maybe in the end she really wanted to live. He remembered the look in her blue eyes that she was afraid of wrong decisions. He remembered seeing her face shut in anticipation of the death event. Peter wanted to tell her that it was the dying maple tree that he wanted to hit.

The failed effort not to hit his wife caused him to lose momentum and hit the tree only hard enough to leave him with bruises. He made the wrong decision trying to avoid her. He should have avoided her when they first met forty two years ago.

Upon her death, the thought that they were separated forever thrilled Peter. He believed in the real world again. It was survivable, he decided while looking down at his wife's torn body. Peter saw a second chance at life that even jail could not dampen.

As he sat beside her body growing cold, a heavy limb from the damaged tree fell and crushed Peter's head. He laid beside his dead wife underneath this dying tree trying to keep from going to sleep. Because, once he went sleep he would find himself beside his wife forever.

Stanley commutes by train to Northern Virginia where he works on budgets. He has had a dozen of his short stories published in national and international small press magazines in addition to several essays and over a dozen book reviews published locally. He is a member of the Riverside Writers and the Virginia Writers Club. Stanley is working on a science fiction book about monsters who may be no more than different looking people.

Of Life, Death, and New Beginnings

Linda Silvey

Storm clouds had rolled in earlier that evening, keeping the moon and stars hidden behind their dark cloak. She knew farmhouses lay out in the distance, but like the sky, were also swallowed by darkness. The only light came from the two headlights on her car that streamed like ribbons just enough for her to see a few feet ahead. Rain poured down the windshield in a steady stream, wipers useless in the unusual torrent.

"Jesus. Nearly eight years of holding back the rain and now you want to dump it on us all at once," she grumbled to herself, wishing she could shake her fists at the sky. Instead, she kept both hands planted on the wheel. Hydroplaning off the road in the middle of nowhere was not on her agenda for tonight. Sheryl Crow's voice singing "All I Wanna Do" streamed out of the radio, helping to ease her tension, but her grasp remained tight.

"Twenty miles left. I can make that. Not a problem," she said, trying to reassure herself. A few minutes had passed before a pair of glaring orbs appeared out of the darkness ahead, expanding their blinding light across her windshield as it finished rounding a curve up ahead. Initially the size of oranges, they quickly grew into the size of basketballs. *Did the lights sway?* She couldn't tell. The growing light seared into her eyes so that she could see nothing else, the darkness now gone. Time froze, spreading its paralysis into her body. The only movement she could make was to tighten her grip on the steering wheel as the light consumed her.

She woke up and instantly looked towards Evan, finding him still sound asleep. The nightmare was becoming more frequent as the wedding day drew near. She was able to hide it most nights, Evan unaware of her sitting up awake with sweating pouring down her face. It had started up soon after their engagement two months ago, the same dream she had had as a child. Elise didn't understand why it had come back to her after all this time.

"Another nightmare?" Tonight wasn't one of them. Elise could make out his shadow next to hers in the dark.

"Yeah. It's nothing, go back to sleep." Instead, she felt him roll over onto his side. He caressed her leg under the covers. "Same old wedding nightmares? We're having a small wedding and you have help from everyone you know. What's to stress about?"

"It's still our wedding and I'm still involved. With so many people helping, I have to make sure all the tiny details are taken care of."

"It wouldn't hurt for you to take a couple days off and relax, you know."

Elise rubbed her temples in frustration. "So I'll have more things to fret over when I come back from my mini-holiday? She didn't why she snapped at him. Her nightmares had nothing to do with wedding plans, but she lied because that was something she couldn't tell him.

"Look, I'm just trying to help," he replied with a touch of hurt in his voice.

"I know. I'm sorry, I shouldn't have snapped at you."

"It's all right. I guess this will be one of those things I'll never understand," he sighed as he rolled onto his back.

Elise smiled and patted his arm. "It's because you're not a woman who's fantasized over her wedding since she was five. Big wedding, small wedding, it doesn't matter. It has to be perfect."

"And that is why I am perfectly happy to be a man." Elise threw her pillow at him.

"Dude, come on. You're getting married in two weeks and we're celebrating your inevitable and idiotic willingness to chain yourself with all of these lovely women and alcohol."

Evan leaned back in his chair and shook the ice that remained in his drink. "This isn't even my bachelor party, Scott."

Scott signaled a waitress who happened to glance at their table. He raised Evan's empty glass. She nodded in acknowledgment, turning her attention to the guy who had just grabbed her butt, slapping his hand away with one hand and managing not to drop the drink tray in her other hand.

"Ha ha! That dude's bold, but it looks like that girl has had that happen to her before. Her tray didn't even tip! And who cares if it's not your bachelor party.

Let's call it your pre-Bachelor party!" Evan didn't feel like partying. The music was too loud, scantily clad women were everywhere, winking, pursing their lips all the while pushing up their breasts through their low-cut tees. The bar brought back memories of when he and Scott met, at a frat party in college. It was a brotherhood founded on girls and alcohol, but it was college so they lived it up until he met Elise a couple years later, then everything changed for him. She didn't party, she didn't really drink, wasn't obsessed with shopping, which was a real shocker, but really, she didn't do much of the things girls did. She fascinated him.

"Geez, man. Don't believe 'em. Married life can't be as bad as they say. Why do you look like you've been sentenced to life in prison?" Evan didn't feel like shouting over the blaring music.

"Can we get out of here?"

Scott frowned, taking in one last look around the bar. "Yeah, sure let's go."

The deafening beat of bass still reverberated through his skull as they stepped out into the street. It felt good to be out of the bar. He blinked as he finished the thought. Never did he expect to say that. It was a sign he was getting older. Evan looked up and down the street for a place where they could hear themselves think. A small café, Monell's, was nestled in between the bars that dominated the block a couple doors down. A red neon sign blinked "Open 24 hours" above the name.

Following Evan's line of sight, Scott then looked at his watch. "11:30. Do you think they'll still be serving food?"

Evan shook his head. If it wasn't alcohol, it was food, or a woman, or something. Always something with Scott. Evan pointed to a smaller decal on the window that read, "24 hour food service."

"Answer your question?"

"Awesome. I like this place already." The woman behind the counter yawned as she straightened from her propped up position on the counter. She banged her hand on the kitchen window to signal the cook and straightened her uniform. Scott made his way to a corner booth near the window and grabbed a menu that was wedged between the glass and napkin holder not bothering to wait for Evan to sit down. The waitress walked over, tapping a pencil against her notepad, annoyed they had bothered to come in.

"What y'all have?"

"Two decaf coffees and I'll have the breakfast omelet with tomatoes, onions, and cheese," Scott said before glancing at Evan. "You want anything besides coffee?" He shook his head no. The woman huffed as she strutted back behind the counter.

"Now, what's your problem?" Scott asked settling into the seat.

Evan sighed. Scott was not a person to beat around the bush. He went straight for it. "I'm not sure Elise wants to get married."

Scott raised an eyebrow. "What? To you or in general?"

"I haven't figured that out yet. I mean, I know she loves me, but she's been…different." He didn't know how to describe how she had been; it wasn't one thing, though it all seemed to point to one definite truth.

"As in bad or just stress? You know how women get about weddings, the whole bridezilla thing and what not. Even as low key as Elise is, I'm sure she's not immune to that whole female targeted epidemic."

He leaned forward. "You know, I can't be exactly sure, but she started acting funny soon after we had gotten engaged. It doesn't make sense though. If she didn't want to marry me, why did she say yes?"

"Girls are funny, man. Maybe she just wants the ring you gave her. It is pretty nice and would go for a huge chunk of change."

"You know she's not like that."

"No I don't. Like I said, girls are funny. They're smart too. If it weren't for their hormonal mood swings giving away their secrets, they'd get away with a bunch of shit."

"If you'd stop flashing your money around you might find yourself a nice girl instead of the gold diggers that have been crawling out of the woodwork." Scott brushed the comment aside with a wave of his hand.

"So have you talked to her about it?"

"Yes and no. I've asked her if there was anything wrong and told me she was stressed about the wedding, getting it perfect," he leaned back in his seat, "maybe I'm over-analyzing this whole thing. She is a bit of a perfectionist."

The waitress returned with their cups of coffee, setting them down in front of them and turning without asking if they needed anything else.

"There you go. You're just overreacting." Evan watched as Scott poured sugar and creamer into his coffee, licking the bit that dribbled onto his finger. He was not helping to ease Evan's mind. Outside, a young couple were walking arm in arm, laughing and ignoring everything around them. Evan remembered when he and Elise were the same way, when the love was new and exhilarating. He knew it wouldn't always be like that, full of romance and surprises, but he still couldn't shake the feeling she was pulling away from him.

"Damn, this is a pretty good omelet. You should have gotten one."

The waitress had come and gone without his notice and Scott was digging into his plate with a voracious hunger.

"What if I'm not overreacting?"

Scott paused from shoveling his next forkful of egg into his mouth, and laid it back down on the plate.

"This is really bothering you, isn't it? Well, I'd say you need to sit her down and talk to her about it," he held up his hand when Evan tried to argue, "Not the

beat around bush conversation. Ask her straight out. It's the only way you're going to get a real answer." He leaned forward. "Or are you afraid of the answer?"

When Scott was focused, he could always hit the bulls-eye of any situation. Evan rubbed his face tiredly.

"I'm not sure. I guess I am. What if she really doesn't want to marry me after all?"

"Listen man, I know me and the guys give you a bunch of crap over her, but really, we're just jealous. You're happy and you have an incredible girl. And trust me, she loves you. If you take anything I say seriously, let it be this: She loves you."

"Yeah, I know she does," he sighed. *But was it enough?*

Elise looked around the room, her eyes adjusting to the darkness. The blankets lay bunched up at the foot of her bed; evidence of a fitful nightmare. A tingle of fear sprang up within her when she recognized the bed was not her own. Dark, repetitive shadows emerged from the wall. Bright and ornate flowers she recalled the gaudy, lavender wallpaper that was blinding to anyone who entered the room in daylight. It wasn't much better at night for they looked like specters, ready to detach themselves from the wall.

September twenty-fifth. Elise propelled herself upright as the date's significance dawned on her. Today was her wedding day. As if to confirm the thought, a flash of light in the corner caught her eye. Her wedding dress hung from a standing mirror; the tiny bead work sparkled against the small rays of moonlight that tickled across the bodice. The mirror scattered the fragmented light across the room.

"Light beams." She said as she wiped the matted hair away from her face. The reflecting light must have triggered her brain to pull that dream from the basement of her mind. That's all it was.

"What?" a sleepy voice asked from the dark. Elise looked over at Deanna's form bundled under the covers of the other bed. Elise realized she had spoken aloud.

"Nothing, sorry to wake you. Go back to sleep."

"Did you have a nightmare or something?"

"Nah. Just woke up. It's nothing," Elise lied.

"That might work on Steph or Jess, but not me. You're not getting cold feet, are you?" Deanna yawned, "Everything's going to be fine today, you know. The perfect wedding." Elise heard a sigh. Happily married with a three year old, Deanna was still a bit jealous of her best friend, though she thought she hid it well from Elise. In truth, she was the envy of all her girlfriends, married or not. Evan had the looks of a movie star: 6'1" with an athletic body, brown, short hair and a jaw line that was the prime example of masculinity. While Elise had to admit his good looks, it was the fact that he understood her, knowing when to push and when to leave her alone with her thoughts, that made her fall in love with him. It couldn't have been more Disney; the perfect fairy tale wedding of which every girl wished for.

"Heck no, I'm marrying Evan. Just a bit of jitters of having to stand in front of everyone. You know I hate to be the center of attention." A soft snort was Deanna's only reply as she rolled away from Elise.

Thankful her friend dropped the matter Elise thought back to her nightmare. *Why now? Was it just because she was getting married or was there another reason?* Elise pushed the covers away and grabbed whatever clothes lay on the nearby chair.

"Where are you going?"

"For a run and to watch the sunrise. Go back to sleep, I'll be back in a bit," she responded quickly. Not wanting to enter the interrogation session she knew would be coming, Elise grabbed her sneakers on her way towards the door.

"Elise-" Deanna started.

"It's just a run, not Runaway Bride; I'd need my dress on for that, so stop worrying. I'll see you at breakfast."

Forty minutes and three miles later, Elise stood looking at the oceanic expanse as the first rays of sunlight broke through the trees behind her,

its rays casting a shimmering sheen across the water. Today was the day that would mark a new chapter in her life; a happy chapter, but this morning's nightmare still stuck with her. *Stop thinking!* It didn't matter how many times she mentally kicked herself, her mind still wouldn't stop. It was the way she was designed. Mediation was lost completely on Elise; she almost had no idea what a blank mind was and envied those who did.

She tried anyways, forcing herself to concentrate on her surroundings. Deep breaths brought the scent of salt, seaweed, and the slightest hint of redwood pine from the forest across the Pacific Coast Highway behind her. It was a place her parents had taken her many times as a child where she would frolic among the giant, red guardians of the mountains, then later, play a game of tag with the ocean's waves. In Elise's mind, it was a harmonious blend of nature's beauty. She exhaled and closed her eyes as the latest wave receded back down the slope, causing the sand to move beneath her half buried feet. The modulating motion of the soft earth created a disorientating sensation which nearly made Elise lose her balance. She dug her feet further into the wet sand, feeling the tiny pricks of small sea crabs struggling to gain control in the shifting ground.

Ten years. It's been ten years. It didn't seem half that long since the day the second law of thermodynamics had chosen her life as its example. "Everything happens for a reason." She had once despised that saying, not because it was, in her opinion, the most clichéd phrase in existence, but for the simple reason that it implied an individual had no control over events in his or her life. It was as if it was society's way of dealing with life's disappointing failures, but for Elise, failure came from a mistake, a lack of proper planning, or an oversight, not something controlled by some unseen force. Elise was not one to crawl into a corner and accept defeat. It had been written into her DNA to look a challenge in the eye and fight as if she had nothing to lose. No other choice was an option.

As time passed, she learned to pick her battles, instead of tackling all of them at once. She now focused on the things around her. The little wonders of life like the tiny hermit crab trekking across the sand or the way the waves eddied along the shoreline were things she used to be in awe of when she was a little girl.

Elise felt a tear roll down her face, but did nothing to wipe it away. It was a tear of mixed emotions: excitement and joy with a strong dose of trepidation. As painful as the last ten years had been she never wanted to forget. The past made her who she was now, despite how painful much of it was. Elise wasn't unhappy; she knew she was marrying the man her father would have wanted her to marry. The only thing that kept the wedding from being perfect was her father's presence.

It was why she had chosen this location. Past and present colliding together with Elise in the middle, hoping the rift in her heart would finally close and make her whole again, merging her happy childhood with her complicated adulthood.

A piercing cry sent a chill down Elise's spine. It all came back in a rush, as if it were happening all over again. She shut her eyes as her lungs grasped for air, her heart clenched tight like a fist ready to burst with unimaginable force. *Was the room moving? Who had screamed: her mom or herself?* Elise didn't know, but as suddenly as it came, the tightness was gone. Her organs struggled to regain their balance. She didn't know how much time had passed, but when she forced her eyes open, she found her mother, tucked into herself on the floor.

Elise rushed to her mother's side, checking the vein on the side of her neck. The familiar 'thump, thump' beat its rhythmic cadence into her fingers.

"She'll be all right. Give her some room," replied the man behind her. His voice carried a disconnect of emotion, as did his face. Elise thought it was something years of training taught; a trick not yet picked up by the woman who stood just beyond the man, uncomfortable and unsure of what to do. In her panic, Elise had forgotten the strangers were in the room.

The coroner, wearing a shabby, navy blue suit, pushed past Elise and knelt next to her mother, fingers pressed into her wrist checking for a pulse. The pungent stench of his cologne hung in the air. His disheveled appearance, from his thinning, unkempt hair down to his scuffed shoes, made it apparent that he was unaccustomed to dealing with the living. In a black pant suit, Elise had to smirk at the ironic choice of color; the petite, slightly plump woman looked no more comfortable in the situation than her colleague.

"She just fainted," he said.

As if on cue, her mother groaned softly. It was a relief. Their relationship was far from close, but she was now the only parent Elise had left, though she would never admit it aloud how much she needed her.

"Adam." Elise almost fainted herself.

"I'm sorry?" The coroner looked up at Elise in confusion.

"My brother," she replied as if the man should already know.

"There's another person in the house?" he asked, his voice revealing a small frustration of not knowing this information beforehand. The shock of news and her mother's fainting was beginning to wear off, her pain ready to erupt from her heart. *Who was he to come in here, tell me my dad is dead, and then have the audacity to have an attitude?*

The coroner was blind to the rage that was brewing inside her. "How old and where is he?"

"He's eight. He's been reading in his room…" her voice broke at the realization she would have to be the one to tell him daddy wasn't coming home.

"He'll have to be told," he said as he guided her mother to the couch. She instantly curled up and began to weep. *Blast that man. Must he state the obvious and further upset her mother?*

50

Aloud she said, "I'll tell him. I think you've done enough, thank you." The woman companion sniffed in disapproval, but Elise ignored it keeping her stern gaze on the coroner who mirrored her expression.

"Yes, well I guess we have. We will leave you to your grief. Our condolences to your family," he replied with a slight nod of his head. Elise wished the pair would hurry up and leave as she was on the verge of crying in front of them. Someone squeezed her hand.

Blinking, the living room vanished and the beach reappeared before her. Elise looked up from the hand that held hers to find Deanna standing beside her, still in her tank top and pajama bottoms of pink and purple polka dots.

"I can't feel him. Today of all days and I feel nothing of him."

"He's here. He's never left you. You probably don't feel him because your emotions are all over the place right now."

"I don't have cold feet," she replied curtly, taking her hand back.

Deanna didn't take her eyes off the water, "Yeah, you told me already. But you're getting married today, and with your dad not here… obviously it's going to be a hard day for you."

Elise walked closer to the water, letting the waves lap against her legs. "I picked this spot so he'd…he has to be here," she mumbled quietly.

Deanna wrapped her arms around her friend in support, hoping to be a small comfort in Elise's internal struggle to be whole.

"Did you have cold feet before you got married?" Deanna pulled away to look at Elise.

"I'd be lying if I said I didn't. It's natural. Actually, I was beginning to worry about you."

Elise looked at her friend curiously, "Worried? Why?"

"Every married person I know have all had a touch of cold feet, including me. You, on the other hand, have been much too calm. If I didn't know you any better, I'd believe you immune."

"But?"

Deanna put her hands on her hips and gave her 'the look'. "But I do know you better than that."

Elise threw her hands up in the air. "So what am I supposed to do? Cry? Freak out? Jump for joy? What?"

"No, I'm not saying that. Though it might help to talk about what you're feeling."

There was no sense in holding anything back now. Deanna was on to her and would continue to be until she teased it out of her. "What would you say if I told you I wasn't sure?"

Deanna took a few steps back towards dry sand and plopped herself down. "I'd say

that's the first honest thing you've said all morning," she said as Elise took a seat beside her.

The waves filled in the silence as Elise tried to piece out her feelings. The sand fell through wiggling toes as she dug her feet in the sand.

"What are you sure about?"

Elise rubbed her face in frustration, unable to come up with an answer.

"Okay, let's try this. Don't think. Just answer yes or no, whichever comes first to your mind." Elise eyed her, puzzled.

"Don't give me that, just do it," Deanna huffed. "Do you love Evan?"

"Yes."

"Are you happy with Evan?"

"Yes."

"Do you want to marry him?"

"Yes."

"Are you scared you'll lose him?"

"Yes."

"Scared that you will end up like your mom?"

"Ye-," she stopped and looked at Deanna who gave her a sad smile. There it was. The truth laid out plain and simple without denial or excuses. The question now was what to do with it, which was much more difficult to answer. Consequences abounded on both sides: Leave Evan at the altar and lose her soul mate, or marry him, but be ever fearful of one day losing him in some tragic accident like her father. Both choices were equally dismal. The further she dug into each scenario eventually resulted in her being alone. *But that was the crux of it all, wasn't it?*

The last ten years had been hard on her mother and harder for Elise to watch. She had long abandoned the thought that her mother would one day snap out of it and find happiness again, though Elise still tried, buying her concert tickets,

52

suggesting ideas to meet people outside of church, hobbies, none of it worked. In Elise's mind, her mother's marriage to her father brought nothing but heartache, something which Elise had already been through once and was not willing to go through again.

"You deserve to happy, Elise. Of any of us, definitely you. It's within your grasp, with Evan. It's not going to be the perfect marriage, no one has that except Disney princesses, but you'll have a good life with him. All you have to do is take it. Look, you've always been the type of person who does your own thing for your own reasons. I can't tell you what to do." Deanna shook her head when Elise tried to protest. "No, this is something you have to work out for yourself. If you decide you'd be happier without Evan then I support your decision. I love you and I want every happiness for you, with Evan, without him, whatever it happens to be. " Elise snapped her mouth closed, frowning.

The pain of her father's death was something she could have never imagined. Grief nearly overtook her, but she found the strength to continue. Elise didn't know how, she related it all to the genetics she was given. A few years of roaming through life in a daze, it all changed when she met Evan. He had breathed life back into her like Prince Charming in Snow White leaving Elise feeling elated and special. She hadn't had that in so long she held on to it as long as she could. Now, a few hours away from her wedding she began to have doubts. No, that wasn't exactly true. The apprehension began shortly after their engagement earlier in the year. Evan had opened her heart when she thought it would never open again, giving her new life and hope for the future, but as the big day drew near she found herself unsure.

Elise sighed. *Why couldn't she let go?* She shook the web of psychoanalysis out of her head and turned to Deanna.

"Breakfast is being set up. Come on, it's going to be a long day and you're going to need food to get through it, whatever you decide," she coaxed.
"Yeah, there had better be a lot of food. I wonder if my dress could hide some of the five pounds I'm about to gain?"

"You'd have to fit into it first."

They both laughed as Deanna dragged her soon to be married friend behind her.

"You're going to rub a hole in that dress if you keep at it," Audrey commented as she pulled her away from the mirror, sitting her down in a nearby chair with a glass of champagne. If it weren't for the fancy dresses, hair and makeup it would seem like just another day with the girls, hanging out watching movies over drinks and girl talk.

She didn't know how long she had tuned out until she was brought back to the present, "Hey, Elise. You're supposed to drink the champagne, not hold it."

"Or wear it." Frantic at Deanna's comment Elise swung the glass away from her and searched her dress for the offending stain. Giggles and snorts told her she had been duped. Again.

"It's really too easy," Deanna said in between fits of laughter. The scowl on Elise's face drew tears from her eyes.

Audrey pointed to the floor. "You're lucky she didn't splash us with the champagne."

"But it would go really well with your dress. You know, give it a uniqueness. Maybe you should consider it." Stephanie held out the bottle of champagne as if to help.

"Yes, that would be so sexy," Elise responded, rolling her eyes.

"I'm sure it would give Evan some thoughts about how the honeymoon is going to go!" Laughter erupted again. If they didn't watch themselves, they would be drunk before Elise walked down the aisle.

A knock on the door brought a halt to the festivities. "Elise? Are you dressed?" Deanna stood up and opened the door to let in her mother while the other girls scrambled to clear away the glasses, evidence which would bring about a lecture to all of them from her own mother. Despite being twenty-eight years old, Elise still tiptoed around her mother as if she were five. The girls were fighting to

hide guilty faces, not immune to her mother's frown. Finding things to suddenly check on, they dismissed themselves, leaving Elise alone with her mother who was standing with her arms crossed. Her mother's frown clashed with the sunny yellow dress she wore.

"Drinking is something you've picked up from your father's side. You couldn't wait until after the ceremony?" her mother stated, clucking her tongue in disapproval.

Elise rolled her eyes as she moved towards the mirror to make sure she hadn't spilled champagne on her dress. She had spent months looking for just the right dress with the right ratios of beading and lace. Nothing ostentatious, but simple, elegant and most of all, flattering. Her broad shoulders were able to pull off a strapless, but her bust line needed help. Made of taffeta, it was a full A-line dress with a lace trim on the bust accented with a sunburst of crystal beading stemming from the pleated side of the dress and expanding across the bodice. The chapel length train finished the dress that made Elise think she were a princess.

"You've never looked more beautiful," he mother beamed approval behind her. "See how pretty you look in dresses? You should wear them more often." Elise sighed. It was an almost perfect, non-criticizing moment, though the remark strangely comforted her. Her mother never changed for anyone or any situation. She said what thought without caring how it was interpreted. Thankfully, it was something she had not inherited from that side of the family.

"Then I lose the shock and awe when I do," she quipped.

"Must you always argue with me when I give you a suggestion?"

"Yes. It's in the daughter handbook."

"Ach." Her mother slapped her playfully across the shoulder. "It is a good thing we got Ryan that tux. I don't think his old suit would fit him anymore."

"A suit and a tuxedo are two different things. A suit is for every day while a tuxedo is for formal events, like my wedding."

Her mom shrugged. "It's all the same to me. Both look much better than raggedy pants and t-shirt," she paused, leaning down to lift up the gown, "Are you wearing all your undergarments?" Elise twirled around, the dress moving out of her mother's grip.

"I'm not five, mom. Everything is where it's supposed to be." In the mirror's reflection, Elise saw her mother's face fall to sadness. *Was she crying?*

"Mom? What's wrong?" With a flick of her hand, she waved Elise's concern away.

"Mother? Don't turn away from me. Please." At her pleading, her mother turned to face her daughter though unable to look her in the eyes. She was crying. The older woman fussed over the skirt of her dress, making sure the beading was fastened properly. A waste of money if one thread was out of place, her scrupulous mother had always said. This emotion was one Elise hadn't seen in nearly ten years. Indifference and criticism she knew all too well.

"My beautiful daughter," she said cupping Elise's face in her hands. Unable to stop them, tears swelled.

"I've been so hard on you especially since…"

"Momma, please. You don't have to." A sharp look silenced what she was going to say next.

"It has only been because I love you. I should have told you that more often. Your father had no problem with that," she smiled, "I love you."

The wedding dress made it a bit difficult to rush into her mother's arms, but she managed it with a force that almost toppled them both to the ground.

"I love you too, Mom. More than anything."

"Easy. You don't want to mess up your make-guess it's too late," she said finding a smudge of mascara as she pulled away to look at her daughter. Laughing, the two women wiped away tears.

"Let's fix this. We don't want to keep everyone waiting." The moment was over. It was not something unexpected. The few times her mother had shown her any feeling it was gone before she could become comfortable with the idea. Once again, the quiet filled the room while her mother wiped off the ruined makeup with tissue and Q-tips.

Holding out the wand her mother said, "Now, let's fix this mascara." Elise grabbed her wrist just as she began to lean in.

"Wha-?"

"Momma." The crying began again. Elise couldn't help it. The nightmare that morning had shaken Elise to the core and she was unable to contain it any longer. All the work done earlier that day by the stylist was undone in a few minutes.

"Am I doing the right thing? Marrying Evan?"

Her mother knelt beside her, wiping her tears away. "Why are you asking me? You know what you want. Don't you?"

"I love him, I know that much, but what if...if he...something happens...if...," she stammered feeling her lungs starve for air as she began to hyperventilate. Gentle fingers lifted her head.

"I know I've made it seem like I regret marrying your father. The pain feels as fresh as was ten years ago. I miss him more now than ever before, but I don't regret it. Your father was a great man and I'm glad he chose me to share his life with. I have two amazing children out of it."

"I can't go through it again."

"People are born and then they die. That's life. Try as much as you want to shut it out, but what kind of life is that? We become who are by who we have in our lives. We are shaped by others as they are shaped by us. Embrace life. Love."

"But you-"

"I've made my choice. Your father is the only man for me. Others don't

 understand and push for me to remarry, but I don't want to. This is how I choose to honor your father."

"By being unhappy? Oh, mother-," she started only to be cut off again.

"Maybe you will understand when you are

older, but this is my choice-No, accept. Don't argue. What makes me happy are you and Ryan. Your happiness is most important now, not mine."

Elise hugged her mother tightly.

"Now, shall we fix this mess you've made?"

"Mess I made, I-," she laughed. For once, she understood her mother's jabbing humor. She was right.

Ryan was waiting outside the door when Elise and their mother stepped out into the hallway.

"Would you stop fidgeting with that tie," they said in unison. Ryan blinked and then rolled his eyes as the women laughed. It was odd to see them getting along, but it was his sister's wedding day so maybe they had made some sort of pact. Elise stepped up to him to fix his tie, loosening it a bit so he could breathe comfortably and then straightened it, all the while grinning from ear to ear.

"Thanks," he said as he peered down at her.

She patted his chest. "You're welcome. You look very handsome."

"You look beautiful. I'm really glad you're happy." He meant it.

"I'm not going to ruin my makeup again," she replied cryptically as she gave him a playful punch. He had no idea what she meant by that. Looking to their mother just made the whole situation more confusing. The look on his face must have given him away because they started laughing again.

"We're women, leave it at that," Elise said as she hooked her arm around his.

"Ready?"

"Let's go."

"How you feeling?"

"Nervous as all hell," he responded, not taking his eyes off the doors at the back of the small church. His palms were beginning to sweat.

"Is this going to be a race of who's going to bolt first?" Scott jabbed him in his side. Evan knew he was trying to get him to relax, but he couldn't help it. He was sure he wanted to spend the rest of his life with her after six months of dating. Elise was slower to come around. He was kind and patient, knowing how her past haunted her.

"I'm not going anywhere."

"Good. For a minute there, I thought I threw eight hundred dollars down the toilet for this tux," Scott replied, tugging at his silver vest underneath the jacket.

Evan finally blinked, turned and clapped his friend on the back, "Don't worry, the way Stephanie's eyeing you, it was the best eight hundred dollars you've ever spent."

The rest of the wedding party was assembled outside the main hall. She caught Deanna's eye and smiled. She smiled back. Elise took a deep breath; behind those doors was her future. Her mother walked ahead of her, without an escort, through the doors of the church held open by a pair of ushers. Everyone in the church stood and turned as the music began to play. She began to sweat from all the attention directed at her.

Her brother leaned down towards her and whispered, "This is worse than graduation, good thing they're all staring at you."

"Is this your way of comforting me?"

"Nah, just getting one last jab in before you become a married woman."

Elise tried not to roll her eyes and kept the smile plastered on her face. "You're seriously not helping right now."

"Relax, sis. You'll make it down the aisle with no problem. We'll do this together," he said with a gentle squeeze of her hand.

"Just take your place with the ushers when we get up there, okay? It's already going to be a crowded marriage with mom nosing around." Her brother nearly choked at her comment, covering it up with a laugh.

It was time. For the first time in her life, she put logic in the back of her mind. She let it all go, focusing on the man who stood waiting for her at the other end of the aisle, shedding not tears of sorrow, but finally, of joy.

Linda Silvey is a thirty-something-year-old female who has rediscovered her love and passion for writing. She has several works of various types – novels, screenplays, short stories and poems – in various stages of creative development. This does not include any of the ideas that frequently and randomly pop in her head at the most inconvenient of times. In 2010, she left Tennessee and returned to her native Californian roots. Most recently, her work has appeared in publications such as Quite Curious Literature, and, of course, Ink Monkey Magazine.

A Pirate's Life

Meredith Bartolo

The pirate didn't know what happened. One minute they were sunbathing off the coast of Spain and the next he was watching as his ship sailed off, abandoning him. He had wondered if this was coming since he had started the Non-Violent Pirate movement, which didn't always go over so well with his crew. Sure, they liked being spared from plank-walking and being dragged through barnacles, but to not be able to do that to others? Honestly though, it was the Robin Hood-ish-ness of the pirates missions that caused the crew to abandon him. They had done their charity work, now they wanted to make it rain.

At first he tried to join other crews, but the economy hit everyone hard and even pirate ships weren't taking newbies. "There's not much luxury left in the high seas." One captain had sighed, before taking a swig of what the pirate could've sworn was seawater. Before he could be sure, the captain waved him away with a gristled old hand and there was nothing to do but leave.

Weeks and months passed, things the pirate had forgotten even existed! He was running out of money since he never really kept much for himself, and knew he needed to get some kind of job. He filled out applications and wrote a resume but it seemed like no one wanted to hire a pirate. They just didn't feel like they could trust him.

"They just don't understand, Rotty." He told his parrot as they ate dinner together. "Maybe I'm not a pirate anymore."

"Squak! Not a pirate! Squak!" Rotty agreed cheerfully and the pirate sighed. He didn't know what to think about that.

Finally the pirate got through to a second interview and he really felt like he had a chance to get this job. *I've had never felt nervous before*, he thought as he smoothed down his hair and adjusted his eye-patch. He didn't know if he liked it, this anxious feeling; actually he was pretty sure he didn't.

"So your last job was being a pirate?" The interviewer asked as he scanned the resume on the desk.

"Aye…but I was a good pirate!" He went on to explain his work and all the practical skills being a pirate afforded him. The interviewer seemed impressed enough so the pirate sat back in his seat, waiting.

"So, I'm sorry, but I do have to ask, is it possible for you to leave your sword at home?" The interviewer pulled a little on his necktie, looking ill-at-ease.

The pirate blushed. He hadn't even realized he was wearing it, it was as natural to him as a second skin or third eye.

"I'm sorry, I just forgot…" He trailed off and the interviewer nodded.

"Well some of the other employees might be, um, concerned if they saw it. Besides, we have a no weapons policy in the office." The interviewer gathered up some papers on his desk and handed them to the pirate, then cleared his throat, "Well, welcome aboard."

"You mean I got the job?" The pirate was at once filled with both dread and elation. Did this mean he wasn't a pirate anymore? As a pirate, he knew it was victory or die, but never surrender. Which was it he was doing now? Somehow it felt like all three.

The interviewer stood up and put out his hand for the pirate to shake, but he just sat there paralyzed, for the first time unsure about his life.

Meredith Bartolo has a masters degree in education, she just doesn't know where it is right now. Despite that, she spends her days encouraging exploration as a teacher. Meredith likes mermaids and dinosaurs, and thinks unicorns are real, but maybe only in Ireland.

The Force Of Will

Richard Radford

Will knew he would be in Tahiti right now if it wasn't for her.

Standing by the inflatable palm trees on the gritty sidewalk of the strip mall, he peered through the tinted windows of Travels-2-Go and watched the scrolling marquee of discounted airfares to exotic locales. Tahiti passed by at $856 and then disappeared forever.

Drooping his shoulders, Will continued along to PawCity next door. Pushing open the soiled door, he cringed as he heard the familiar bell and was assaulted by the odor of wood chips and imprisoned animals. Barks, mewls, piercing squawks. Lonely old cat ladies. Delinquent sales clerks. A couple of dupes like him, no doubt buying hypoallergenic kibble and deworming medication on a Thursday afternoon instead of lying next to mind-blowing women drinking Mai Tais on a beach in Tahiti.

Sarah could have told him the dog had so many medical problems. On the first date, even. He might have minded then, and then again maybe he wouldn't have. But at least she should have given him the information. Up front. Of course then she would have had to tell him she would move in with him five months later, stay for two years, and then suddenly leave and abandon the defective dog after finding her "dream job" on the west coast and some new jerk who owned two cars.

To be precise, Will didn't know for sure if the jerk had two cars. But on Sarah's Facebook account there they were, standing at the ocean next to some expensive-looking convertible with a vanity plate that read "CARTWO." It only stood to reason that its counterpart was waiting for its mate back in the driveway of some luxury condo.

After checking out, he had to fight the rush hour traffic, which had become much worse since he was forced to make the stop at PawCity. He thought enviously of his coworkers who hadn't had to make that stop. All the people in the world who hadn't had to do it. Billions of them. Literally. None of them had to. Just him.

As Will pulled into his driveway, he wondered what kind of a person needed two cars. Maybe if you had a job that required a truck or something, but the guy didn't look like the type who had ever been forced to work a day in his life, let alone hard labor.

Will checked the mail, but of course the box was empty of anything but bills. The grass needed to be cut. The siding needed pressure washing. The windows were smeared opaque with dog nose prints. Maybe after preparing the special dietary meal and applying the deworming medicine he would find time for all of those household chores before having to rush to bed so he could get up and go to work so he could pay for all of the special dietary meals and deworming medicine he couldn't afford.

Yeah right.

The dog was waiting for him by the deep scratches on the doorjamb that would need to be repaired before he got his security deposit back if he could ever get a nicer place that accepted dogs. It wagged its tail obsequiously and limped to his side. No one wanted to pet anything geriatric. That was what they made nursing homes for.

He filled the bowl with the overpriced food, added some warm water, and led the dog to it. Its eyes were probably going too, and Will prayed they had yet to invent canine contact lenses. God knew what those would cost.

After the protracted wrestling match forcing the dark medicine down the dog's throat, Will began to drink. Why it wouldn't swallow the medicine was anyone's guess. It ate garbage. It ate the neighbor's freshly planted caladium bulbs right out of the soil. It even nipped the neighbor's kid supposedly, though the brat had shot it with a BB gun before the attack, and Will was forced to defend it. A BB was still lodged under the skin on its hip, which had never been removed because the vet said it would be fine. Which was also fine with Will, ever since he had to pay thousands of dollars for surgery after the dog ate his razor.

Will continued to drink long after he checked Sarah's Facebook. She was "going to mexico for the weekend :D". Her numerous friends had offered up their "Olé!"s and "party time!"s and "Drink a corona for me!"s. She had pleaded with him to keep the dog. They supposedly didn't allow dogs where she was moving. And there she was next to the convertible again, though the license plate wasn't visible, so maybe it was "CARONE," identical to its sequel. Apparently they don't allow dogs to go to Mexico for the weekend with a jerk with two identical convertibles any more than they allow dogs in California.

He worked through most of the bottle of bourbon reclined in his chair. The dog limped up a couple of times, and he shooed it away. It didn't give up. It never gave up. In its final attempt it rested its node-covered head on his thigh. By that time Will had forgotten to eat and passed out, his hand motionless in mid stroke on the coarse fur behind its ears.

Will woke up in the scratchy sunlight groggy and itchy. His forearm was coated in thin streaks of blood, with little black flecks mixed in. One leapt off him into the blurry room.

Fleas.

There was no doubt about it. A few were drowning in the glass of melted ice and bourbon on the side table. The decrepit beast had slunk off to its ruined blanket in the corner, and barely acknowledged Will scraping at its hair, weakly tapping its tail against the floor. Sure enough, there were fleas. It was lousy with them.

He had just enough time to grab a quick shower before stomping out to his car and joining the herd rushing to work. All day long in his cubicle he reflexively scratched at his scalp and his arms, and could feel the presence of the fleas. Even if he was just imagining them crawling along his spine, he knew they were waiting for him at home, invading the carpet and raiding the pantry and chewing holes in the flesh of that wretched creature and fucking on his recliner.

As usual he skipped lunch, and spent the half hour sucking on the stale mints from the reception desk and staring out the window at the cramped parking lot with the crooked lines, a few sad firs leaning over his aging car in the only space that was ever available when he got there, dripping sap that was impossible to remove onto his windshield. Why the trees were allowed to continue their meaningless existences was anyone's guess. Today his reverie failed to keep his

attention, and every few seconds he would feel the prick of fangs at his neck.

Just after four, Laura came to his cubicle and leaned on the edge of the tan fabric walls.

"Workin' hard?" she asked, straightening her creased blouse and smiling.

"Always," Will said, sitting up rigidly, averting her eyes and looking at the clock on the wall over her shoulder.

"Listen, me and a couple of the girls are going out for happy hour at the Lounge. Want to come?"

Will was already shaking his head disappointment even before she had finished talking.

"You know, I'd love to Laura, but I've got this issue with the dog to take care of."

"Oh. OK...I hope it's not anything serious?"

"No, no, but it needs to be done," he said, holding up his hands towards her with the wrists touching. "My hands are tied."

"Oh, OK," Laura said. "Well, if you change your mind—"

"Can't be helped," he said.

"We'll be there till seven or so."

Will shook his head slowly until she left, and then furiously clawed at the nape of his neck. He could feel them there, feeding.

On the drive to the strip mall, he repeated the words he had spoken—the only ones all day—over and over, in a kind of mantra. He explored all of the promise of the missed night out, where it could have taken him. To a place of ecstasy. To a place of utter calm. To a place where fleas weren't king and anything was possible.

He hurried by Travels-2-Go without looking in the window, and pushed one of the inflatable palm trees out of his way. PawCity had an entire aisle dedicated to poison, nauseating close-ups of the invisible world of invasive pests crawling along the labels of the tubes and boxes. It could be worse, Will reminded himself, but then realized he'd probably go home and see the dog so thick with ticks and lice he would have to sell his car to take care of the problem.

Already ashamed to be buying the dozen flea-killing products, Will spent his time in line wondering if he could just use the dog shampoo on himself as well. He had bought an extra bottle, but the thought of asking the sixteen-year-old girl behind the counter made his heart race and his eyes lose focus.

It didn't greet him at the door as usual when he arrived home, and was still lying on the ruined blanket in the corner. Will set the bag of poison down and stood over the dog. He nudged it with his foot. Nothing. He leaned down and stared closely into the open, unseeing eye. Pressing his ear against the coarse, furry ribcage, he momentarily forgot about the fleas, though they had probably decided their meal was finished there.

Will stood up decisively, moving in a practiced routine. It was one he had followed in his mind hundreds of times, and now when it came time he was magnificent. He gently lifted it up, along with the blanket it had destroyed from months of sleeping and chewing on it, and carried it out through the back of the kitchen. He crossed the tall grass of the backyard to the little rusty shed. Next to it was a crater, not quite square, about four feet deep. Kneeling in the grass, he lowered it into the ground and immediately began to push the loose dirt into the hole. The shovel was still leaned up against the shed, and he used it to scoop the rest of the dirt over the blanket he would have to replace now. It was OK, he reminded himself, it was already ruined.

He stood up, respiring heavily and brushing the dirt from his forearms. Barely taking a pause to look down at the grave, Will headed around the side of the house and directly to his car. He backed out of the driveway without looking, humming to himself and tapping the steering wheel.

The strip mall lot was filling up with post-work shoppers, but Will was lucky enough to find a place to park right by the storefront that wasn't a handicapped space. Looks like my luck is turning around, he thought. He slowed as he walked up to the tinted windows of Travels-2-Go. Tahiti was back, at $845.

Will continued along the sidewalk, opened the door and jaunted in, walking straight up to the counter with confidence.

"Yes sir, how can I help you today?" the sales clerk asked brightly.

"I need to buy a dog," he said, pointing to the wall of desperate creatures rattling their cages.

Richard Radford's fiction has appeared in The Ampersand Review, A Cappella Zoo, Pear Noir!, Sex and Murder Magazine, Jersey Devil Press and other literary journals. He currently lives in Alaska and works as the staff writer for a weekly newspaper

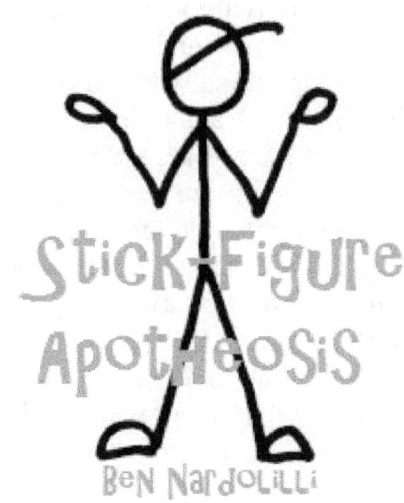

Stick-Figure
Apotheosis

Ben Nardolilli

Exclamation Point!
       Bundle of bright light,
Explosion!
       Perfect steps
At right angles, deadly,
       Everyman rises, climbs,
Trips,
       The dastardly shin,
And he falls forever, never
       Even hitting the ground
Of these interesting stairs.

Ben Nardolilli is a twenty-four year old writer currently living in Arlington, Virginia. His work has appeared in Houston Literary Review, Perigee Magazine, Canopic Jar, One Ghana One Voice, Baker's Dozen, Thieves Jargon, Quail Bell Magazine, Elimae, Poems Niederngasse, Gold Dust, Scythe, Anemone Sidecar, The Delmarva Review, Black Words on White Paper, Cantaraville, and Mad Swirl. In addition he was the poetry editor for West 10th Magazine at NYU and maintains a blog.

Uncle, in a Bad Place

Alana I Capria

1

Uncle, in a bad place, only smells sulfur. Everything runs free like egg yolks. He touches the wall moldings and loses his fingers to the infinite number of hidden mouse traps. The carnivorous springs snap at anything made of meat. Uncle tries to avoid the floor but it is difficult. He cannot hold onto the ceiling. It is a wet cheese texture. He grabs hold of the drips and the ceiling pulls. Where are the windows? Uncle runs his hands across the scalloped floorboards, trying to find glass panes. There is molten glass. His palms brush the liquid and come away.

2

The hallways are a raw yellow. Uncle stumbles through beetle nests. The bugs try to crawl through his ears. Vacant shells rattle around his head. He turns this way and that, smacking his face to unclog the canals. Uncle worries about dung beetles. They burrow into his feet when he stops to sleep. He can feel them now, drilling through the soles. He imagines the crisscross tunnels, their small hives and the larval children growing inside. Uncle punches the walls but there is always another wall behind the first. They hum when he hits. They spit up peas.

3

Uncle finds a dark door. Everything looks like an exposed negative. He makes out a bit of light. Inside is a single straitjacket throw on the floor. The room is not dirty but littered with thumbtacks. Uncle has no shoes. He walks across the chamber on his tiptoes. His heels bleed. Hands come out of the floorboards and wrench his nails off. Unseen mouths crunch beneath him. Uncle remembers a show that was plagued by sandworms. Everyone was dead. He worries about the iron's smell. It reeks too much of un-bathed flesh and not enough of blood.

4

Uncle finds another room that is made up entirely of white blinds. Drywall and blinds. He opens and closes the blinds with a loud clicking noise. He keeps time to the shutters. Something bangs against the walls' outsides. Uncle finds a piece of paper in the corner. It is rolled across one end. Keeping his eyes closed, Uncle sketches his face. When he looks, the drawing is of a waterfall and a terrible pair of eyes just beneath the spray. Uncle's flesh burns from the light. He runs from one wall to the other. He jumps into the corners and ricochets across the floor.

5

Gloved hands serve Uncle a box of bones. He picks through the calcified pieces, trying to find the bones that should belong to him. Some of the bones are too weak. They splinter in his hands. To hide the evidence, he snorts up the dust. The powder burns his nose and throat. Uncle grimaces. Some of the bones claw and bite at at his wrists. *You must not let the white get dirty*, a voice says. Uncle turns his hands around to avoid brushing the blood across the bones. The bones scream and writhe. They chitter to him. They form a cage and keep Uncle inside.

6

Uncle lands in a room that smells like springtime. He pricks his tongue and waits for flowers to grow. A light rain starts in the center of the room. It moves to the corners. Soon, there are Noah's ark caliber rains. Uncle drifts in this domestic sea. He washes from molding to molding. Eggs drop from the ceiling and land around him. They float in the tidal foam. Uncle gathers the eggs beneath his arms and hoists himself onto this unsteady raft. He drifts around the room, barely afloat. A beaming light appears in the rain. Soon Uncle stands in a arid desert.

7

Uncle gets covered by cheese. It is the powdered kind. It sticks to his hair. Mice come to eat the strands. Soon, Uncle is bald. The mice leave. Uncle is hungry. He licks the ground, trying to lift up some of the cheese. It does not taste like cheddar but Gruyère. The milkiness makes him itch. Uncle runs up a spindly flight of stairs. The metal groans around him. The railing creak and stretch. *They do not like to be walked upon*, the steps tell him. They bite his feet as he runs. The railings come apart and kick at his knees. It is a long fall to reach the bottom.

8

Uncle meets a god of death. The hermaphrodite creature hangs from a noose born out of fruiting tree. *You are not welcome here*, the god says. Its genitals move when it speaks. Its mouth is overgrown and fat. Uncle backs away. The fruits crack in half, revealing small people kept inside. They hiss and moan. *Where are you going? Harvest us*, they shout. The death god is a skeleton with a fleshy head. It swings from the noose, kicking its feet to gain momentum. Soon, it swings so quickly the fruit fall from the vibrations. *Take that*, the death god says.

9

Uncle paints himself sepia. He wants to be aged. He touches his hair and wishes for gray. These staircases are too much. He finds plucked chickens on each flight. They peck at his abdomen, drawing honey from his pores. Uncle picks the chickens' up and swings them around in a single rotation. Their necks break. The chickens keep clucking. Uncle makes himself wings out of chicken wattles. He eats the breasts raw. The salmonella tastes like beef gravy. Uncle climbs in and out of picture frames. He waits for the beasts to hang him over the master's bed.

10

Uncle drinks from a hamster's water bottle. He swipes the ledge of a bricked up window and eats a handful of melted Brie. Uncle eats crackers made of his own dried skin. They have the same crunch as pig skins. Maybe not as much fat. But definitely the same roasted lacquer. Uncle dips himself into an acid vat. All this to expose the solidity of his skeleton. The stairs whimper as Uncle passes. The walls shudder and the air runs dry. *It smells like summer*, Uncle says and slips through cracks. There is a painted room he must get to. Only he knows the way.

Alana I. Capria (born 1985) has an MFA in Creative Writing from Fairleigh Dickinson University. She resides in Northern New Jersey with her fiancé and rabbits.

Traipsing through Sunday those dapper youths,
Wane and Suited, richly shoeless,

Swirl in spring a newborn airlight,
parading through the slush of the yard.

An elderly sentinel nods in his crooked ladder-back,
adrift in eyelid skybursts of blue

Too fuzzy and spangled to fear,
And the measured ticks of a cardiac clock...

The grounds of the manor soak in the wake
Of a grieving tempest's tantrum where

Ivy From Afar

Tariq Shah

Well-hid in the garden plaid,
Wet scents snuff the jeers.

April's beamcraft scaffolds the day,
The maple leaves mingle and curl,

A ring of blonde sisters skip in elliptical circles,
glazed and beguiled by blue blood sugars,

Squinting above as a mute rook sky rides,
Convinced the white magic is near.

Where was I?
It is difficult to recall–

Perhaps it was upstairs,
In the rugged basement of heaven

paralyzed in the glue of the hush,
the leer of the wind at the windows

flared in mind the exquisite quiet
I savored before the sharp lemon rapping at my door.

Tariq Shah a writer currently living and working in Chicago. He composes short and long fiction, as well as poetry. Having recently returned from living in Moatize, Mozambique, for the past two years, he is appreciating the curiosities of personal readjustment to the 1st world.

The Casserole War at Little Hope Baptist Church

Paul M. Dillingham

The Breedlove family owned six hundred acres of land in eastern Kentucky. This holding was located between the Big Hope and Little Hope Rivers. The Hope flowed south until it reached a high side in the Appalachians, where it divided into two streams. The Little Hope was not wide or deep; it was slow and meandering and in the heat of July and August it mostly dried up. The local wags said, "It is too wet to plow and too thick to drink." This did not matter to the Breedloves for they did not farm. Their six hundred acres were mostly hills. The richness was not in the soil, it was what lay underneath – coal.

Justin Breedlove was an excellent business man. He did not sell his land, he leased it to mining corporations. Besides the rent, he collected a payment on each ton of coal that was mined. This made him a rich man, but not a good parent. Their only child Homer grew up spoiled, pampered and undisciplined. He was constantly at odds with all authority and found himself in Judge Peabody's court for the seventh time in four months.

The judge was fed up with Homer and said, "I order you to serve six months in the county jail or you can join the U.S. Marines and leave this county in peace. It is your choice and you have 30 seconds to decide."

Homer replied, "I'll take military service." The judge thundered, "I didn't say military, I said U. S. Marines." Homer agreed and the charges were dismissed.

Homer rode the bus to Knoxville and enlisted. He was sent to Quantico, Virginia for his basic training. Marine training is rugged and designed to break a man down and rebuild him into a marine. Homer might have failed; instead he responded and became a man, semper fi, gung-ho, all spit and polish. He asserted himself as the leader of his platoon. When assignments came out, Homer drew a plum. He was sent to the American Embassy in Paris, France, as a guard.

His first week on guard duty he saw a beautiful red-haired, green-eyed young lady leave the building. He was smitten. He found out that her name was Marie Montreau and she was a receptionist in the Consular Section. Each day as she left work Homer would give her a big smile and a salute. One thing led to another and they began to go out on dates. Homer wanted this French beauty. Marie wanted Homer, but their goals were far apart. Homer wanted to sleep with Marie. Marie wanted Homer to marry her and take her to the United States. Homer just wanted to enter the promised land. Marie had had lovers – she was not shy, but she had bigger plans. She let him see and touch, but he was forbidden entry.

Homer gave in and proposed. Marie insisted on being married in the United States. A visa was arranged for Marie. She wanted to make sure she was in her promised land before Homer entered and conquered France.

Homer had a tragic accident in Paris.. A taxi driver ran a red light and struck Homer. His foot was crushed and it had to be amputated. The marines didn't need a soldier missing a foot, so Homer was given a discharge. Marie had to delay her plans. She had damaged goods, but this made no difference. Marie was going to marry Homer because of what she misheard.

While they were courting, Homer told her about how much coal his family had. Marie thought he said "gold" and she was determined to get her share. She was not happy when she learned the truth. Maybe this was the cause of the unhappiness that developed.

Homer's parents were members of the Baptist Church. They wanted one nearby, so they gave land on a bluff overlooking the Little Hope River. When the church was built, they put up a sign proclaiming the name – Victory Baptist Church. Most of the 25 or so who attended the church were older than their fifties. When a storm tore off the name "Victory," no one bothered to replace it. The locals began calling it Little Hope Church and the name stuck, even if the sign didn't.

Justin and Cora missed the wedding because they missed an S curve and wound up in the Big Hope River. They didn't survive. Homer became the president of Breedlove Mining and Marie was pleased with her husband's position and apparent wealth, even if coal was not gold.

The couple was learning things about each other that had not come to light. Marie had learned that Homer had an uncomplimentary nickname. The locals called him Fort Knox Breedlove because it was as difficult to get money out of Homer as it would be to get the gold out of Fort Knox.

Homer was enamored with Marie's stunning beauty, but there was one thing he found out about her after the marriage. She had a temper as fiery as her red hair and it showed up in the second month of their less-than-blissful marriage. She asked her husband to buy her a new car, a Cadillac, no less. He countered with the offer of a Chevy pickup stored in a barn. He even said he would paint it any color she wanted. Homer slept in the spare room that night.

The next morning Homer upped the offer and promised her a new set of tires and to have the AM radio fixed on the truck. Marie threw a tantrum – she also threw the coffeepot and scrambled eggs at Homer. The eggs weren't scrambled until they hit upside Homer's head. That night Homer slept on the screened-in porch.

When Parson Henry Hatfield married them in Little Hope Church, he pronounced them husband and wife till death do them part. This looked like it might come sooner than later. The neighbors who lived near the Breedloves would, after their supper, take chairs into the yard so they could listen in on the arguments between Marie and Homer. Not only were there words, there were plate-throwing, glass-breaking confrontations. Some of the neighbors learned how to curse in French. There was general disappointment when winter set in.

After six months of less than joy and happiness, to say nothing of love, Marie went to see lawyer Lawrence Ledbetter about a divorce. She was sure she could get a better settlement in court than she could get from Homer.. Now Connie Sue McCoy was the secretary for Lawyer Ledbetter and was the very soul of discretion, except she had goo-goo eyes for Homer. Connie Sue sent word to Homer about Marie's intentions and that night, even with the window and doors closed, a huge argument could be heard all the way to Little Hope Church where there was a prayer meeting going on. Connie Sue was present and added her "tsk, tsk" to the domestic dispute.

The next morning Marie Montreau Breedlove was dead. Sheriff Freeman Oglesby could find no outward cause, so he ordered an autopsy. This revealed Marie had died of a burst artery in her brain, brought on by extreme agitation.

Homer was now a widowed man so Connie Sue thought he must be lonely and needy. She baked a ham and egg casserole, an apple pie and some yeast rolls. She didn't want to seem to be too forward, so the food was put in a picnic basket and set on Homer's front porch. She made sure her name was on the basket, just so Homer could return it to the proper person.

Now Connie Sue wasn't the only woman at Little Hope Church who had designs on Homer – so did Pearly Mae Hodgekiss. She was a widow herself and felt she knew better than anyone what Homer needed. She was attractive and could cook as well as Connie Sue. A tuna casserole, cherry pie and a pan of cornbread showed up on Homer's porch with a note of condolences signed by Pearly Mae.

This competition between the two ladies went on for two months. Homer put on fifteen pounds. He was surely enjoying this single life. He had ham and eggs, chicken, macaroni and cheese casserole, even shepherd's pie. One old biddy at Little Hope Church said, "Them gals are gonna casserole Homer to death."

They almost did. Connie Sue came by one day with her food for Homer and someone else had been there before her. There was a cake with chocolate icing on a plate with a glass cover over it. She read the name taped to the cover. "That no-good hussy, Pearly Mae, is trying to beat my time; I'll fix her wagon."

Connie Sue made a stop at Faye Tarbell's Quick Stop Market and bought four packages of Ex-Lax. Faye commented, "You must have a serious blockage." Connie sue answered, "I do, but I am about to eliminate it."

She went home and melted the Ex-Lax into a paste. She hurried to Homer's, scraped off the chocolate and applied her own special icing. This might make Homer uncomfortable, but he wouldn't be eating any more of Pearly Mae's cakes.

The next day Homer came by the Quick Stop and told Faye, "I need some Pepto Bismol – I got the trots real bad." Faye Tarbell put two and two together and mentioned this to her best friend, Pearly Mae.

Pearly Mae said, "That bitch ain't gonna get the best of me." She fumed about this for a few minutes and Faye Tarbell slid a bottle of syrup of ipecac across the counter and said, "Connie Sue was in here earlier and bought some tea bags – said she was gonna make some sun tea."

Pearly Mae drove by Homer's and sure enough, there was a whole gallon of sun tea seasoning on the porch along with a picnic basket. She put the ipecac in the tea and reasoned it would make Homer sick – sick of Connie Sue's cooking.

The next day Homer put a sign on his porch: NO MORE FOOD ACCEPTED. He stopped by Faye Tarbell's store and bought more Pepto Bismol. The one thing Pearly Mae and Connie Sue did not know was why Homer was away from home so much. In fact he was visiting a widow over in Sparrow Hollow. She didn't cook much, but cooking wasn't why Homer spent time with her!

The climax of the casserole war happened on Sunday night at Little Hope Church. There was a pot luck supper. Connie Sue and Pearly Mae arrived at the same time. First there was a contest of stares, then things got downright unfriendly.

Pearly Mae hissed, "Backstabbing bitch." Connie Sue rejoined with "Whore of Babylon." Pearly Mae swung her purse and hit Connie Sue upside her jaw. The blow caused Connie Sue's false teeth to fly out of her mouth and fall on the steps of Little Hope Church. No one knew she had false teeth. Connie Sue grabbed Pearly Mae by the arm and tried to bite it. The best she could do was give it a good gumming. Each grabbed a handful of hair and a wig came off Pearly Mae's head, showing a big bald spot she had covered up. There were a lot of grunts, screams and spit flying.

Parson Hatfield tried to separate the two just as Pearly Mae let go with a high kick. It caught the Parson in his privates and he went down on his knees. It looked like he was praying, but the words coming out of his mouth were not the words God wanted to hear. Deacon Ben Barnholder stepped in and got a finger in his eye. He joined Parson Hatfield on the ground amen-ing some of the same words the Parson had used.

Little Hope Church lost two of its "sisters," but it gave the rest enough gossip `to last a year. Amen!

Paul M. Dillingham is properly seasoned and aged to perfection.
The stories he writes are sparked from real life. In his, he's been there and
done that for just about everything. (The circus is still just a rumor.)
Now, he's a little more settled; he lives with his wife in Nashville, TN.

DoctOr's Things

The lock clicked. Jordan twisted the knob slowly, grinning. The door opened.

He glanced at Casey. "Told ya."

Casey eyed the interior of the garage, nodded at the door that led into the house. "What if that one's locked?"

"Who the fuck locks the door leading out of the garage *and* the door leading from the garage to the house?"

"Someone who's careful. Someone who knows there are people like you out there."

"People like *us*, Tinkles."

"Don't call me that. And this was *your* idea."

"Yeah, and you coulda stopped me anytime you wanted."

Casey scratched his chin. His glove made a muffled, grating sound as it grazed across his skin. He had forgotten to shave that morning.

"Shouldn't we be wearing masks or something?"

"Yeah. 'Cause so many people can see over that fence."

"They could've seen us climbing over it."

"We snuck in through the back, retard. You know what's back there? A fucking *lake*."

"People fishing."

"Drinking beer and watching the little fishies. Fuck 'em."

"They could ID us, Jordan."

"They could give a rat's ass. Come on." He slipped inside.

Casey followed, the duffle bag he carried smacking against his leg. They made it halfway across the garage before Jordan stopped, turned around, and stared at his friend for a second. Then he walked back and closed the door.

"Dipshit," he said, passing Casey on the way back.

They reached the other door. Jordan didn't hesitate; he grabbed the knob and twisted. The door swung open, squeaking a little. Casey winced at the noise, certain that someone passing by on the street could hear it. When no one yelled for them to stop, they went in.

They stood in Dr. Fielding's kitchen. The linoleum floor had been cleaned recently; Jordan's sneakers squeaked as he walked across it, as if it was his, as if he had strolled through this kitchen many times before.

"Should we close the curtains?"

"That's the backyard, Tinkles. No one's out there."

"Don't call me that. I meant, the curtains on the front window."

The kitchen was separated from the front living room by a low brick wall and carved railing, the latter merging with the ceiling in an ornate fixture that had probably cost more than either of the intruders made in a month. The window opened on a trimmed front lawn, which led to a smoothly paved residential lane. A sign notified passersby that the area was patrolled by a Neighborhood Watch.

Jordan shrugged. "I kinda like it open. The risk turns me on."

"Shut up."

"Seriously. Remember Janet? The brunette, short hair, the one my cousin thought looked like a man with big tits? She got me hooked on that voyeurism stuff. Liked to bang in public. Outside, even. It's quite a thrill. You should try it sometime, Tinkles."

"Stop that. It's been three years."

"Yes. But you were *eighteen*, dumbass. Who the *hell* pisses their pants at eighteen?"

"I was sick."

"You were drunk. And so was that girl. But she wasn't *that* drunk. Can't say I'd blame her. That wasn't the kind of liquid she was expectin' to come out of there."

"Shut the fuck up."

"Whatever." Jordan picked up an envelope off of the counter. "Huh. Even rich doctors get Publisher's Clearinghouse, I reckon. Wonder if he's ever entered."

"You're sure he won't be back?"

"Positive. He's at the hospital all day. I see him there, every fucking day, *all* fucking day."

"And you're *positive* there's no alarm?"

"Goddammit, Tinkles. We've gone over this, ain't we?"

"Yeah, but…"

"Yeah but *what*? I overheard him myself—his alarm was on the fritz, it kept going off, the cops kept coming out, and so he just got rid of it. I laughed my ass off when I heard him tell that story. Trust me, I fucking *remember it*."

"Okay."

At the end of the kitchen was a small dining area. The table could easily seat a dozen guests. To the right of the table was another living room, this one decorated to look like a library or study lounge, except for the big-screen plasma TV hanging on the wall. The television was as large as the front window in the bungalow Jordan was raised in.

To the left of the table was a hallway that branched. One branch led to the front living room; despite his cockiness earlier, Jordan decided to leave that room for last. No sense having someone spot them *before* they'd searched the rest of the house. Another branch of the hallway led to other rooms—perhaps a *real* study, an office like all rich folks have. The third branch led to some elegantly-carpeted stairs, which led up to a small landing, then turned out of view.

"Upstairs or straight?" Jordan asked.

"Huh?"

"You wanna go down this hall here, see what he's got on this floor, or you wanna go upstairs?"

"Do you think he got another system installed?"

Jordan turned. "What?"

Casey was biting his lip, eyes darting nervously to the front window, still partially in view. "Do you think he got another alarm system installed? You

know, after his first one broke?"

"It broke *Monday*. He wouldn't have gotten another system installed in just two fucking days."

"Rich people can do anything, Jordan."

"Tinkles, I swear to God…"

"Don't call me that, okay? I'm serious

here. This is a nice house; if he's got stuff worth stealing, he's got stuff worth protecting. *You* taught me that, Jordan, remember? Rule Number One: If there's something worth stealing in a place, there's something worth protecting in it."

"I know what I taught you, dipshit. Here's Rule Number Two, or whatever fucking number we're on now: Even rich people can't perform miracles. Got it?"

"Yeah."

"I want you to *get it*, Tinkles. Don't just pretend with me. Do you trust me or not?"

"Jordan—"

"Tinkles—"

"I get it. I trust you. I'm just nervous, okay? I'm just nervous. We've never broken into a house like this before. This place is…it's *nice*."

"So's the money he's got stashed in a safe somewhere."

"He told you that?"

"I'm a fucking *janitor*, Tinkles. The doctor doesn't tell me shit. I overhear things. And even then, I doubt he'd go around telling people he's got money stashed away. He's rich—it goes with the territory. You said it yourself: a house this nice, there's something worth our while in here. Guaranteed. But we won't get it if you don't trust me one hundred percent."

"I trust you, Jordan."

"Okay then. So: straight or upstairs?"

"Straight, I guess." His eyes darted to the front window, then back to his friend.

"You sure, Tinkles?"

"Yeah. And don't call me that."

Jordan nodded, taking the duffle bag from Casey's hand. He turned and walked down the hall. There were no decorations on the walls, no pictures of a wife or kids. Jordan had checked Dr. Fielding's hand just the day before—no wedding band. He'd been half afraid the doctor had simply forgotten to wear it that day, or had taken it off for some reason. Odd, that a rich doctor should be single. Probably he was gay.

There were four doors opening off the hallway. The first led into a closet, which held nothing exceptional—a vacuum cleaner, some linens, various cleaning supplies, some cardboard boxes that contained photo albums. Jordan flipped through the first album. There were several young women, perhaps half the doctor's age. So he wasn't a fag after all. Most of the women were the kind Jordan could only hope to get on a Saturday night, at closing time, and even then if his hair was parted just right and the girls weren't really looking for quality.

Fucking doctors.

He opened the other boxes; they all contained photo albums too. Some were actual albums—like the kind Jordan's mother kept, where you peeled back the plastic covering and placed the photo on a sticky piece of paper—and some were picture holders from Wal-Mart. None of the photos, however, looked like any prints Jordan had gotten from Wal-Mart.

The doctor probably had his own darkroom; hadn't Jordan overheard something about photography once? The doctor liked to chat with the nurses. Where would the darkroom be? A basement? He hadn't seen a door in the kitchen, aside from the one they'd come in through. They'd have to check the garage more carefully on their way out.

Jordan picked up some lose pictures, leafing through them. There were a lot of women. Some of them looked older—not in age, but in era. One girl had a haircut straight from the eighties, and fake tits to match. So the doc had been playing the field for some time. Jordan smiled. His kinda guy.

"We can't get anything for photos, Jordan."

Jordan put the pictures back in the box, and set the box back with the others. "No, Tinkles, we can't, can we? Goddamn, I have to say the doc has gone up in my estimation. He's a fucking player."

"Good for him. Can we move on? We've been in this closet ten minutes already."

"Patience, Tinkles. Can't miss anything. Although I kinda feel guilty about stealing from him now. But you know what—he'll still have plenty of money in the bank. He can get laid with that, no sweat. We'll even leave him a couple good suits. Don't wanna cock-block the son of a bitch."

Jordan closed the door and went to the next one, on the same side of the hallway. It already lay open, revealing the nicest, largest bathroom he had ever seen.

"Jesus," Casey whispered.

"Yeah." The tiled floor featured some alternating pattern of stripes; it hurt Jordan's head to try and figure it out. The walls took up the same theme. Above the sink was a wall-length mirror, and opposite that was the shower. Whenever the doc stepped out of the shower, before he grabbed a towel, he could look at himself. Probably smile, too. Flex a little.

Jordan smiled as he approached the toilet. "We should take a dump in it."

"What?"

"Leave him a little souvenir."

"Can't they, like, do DNA testing or something?"

"Of course, Tinkles. I wasn't serious."

Still, it was tempting.

He walked to a small cabinet beside the toilet and opened it. There were six shelves, each lined with bottles of medicine—mostly prescription stuff, some over-the-counter shit—arranged alphabetically. All labels faced out; not one bottle was crooked.

"Sweet Jesus," Jordan said, and began sweeping the bottles of medicine into the duffle bag.

"What are you doing?"

"We can get good money for this shit, Tinkles."

"What if he needs that to…to live or something?"

"When he gets home and sees he's been robbed, the first thing he's gonna wanna do is pop some pills. He'll come in here, see he doesn't *have* any, and get all of his prescriptions refilled."

"What if he has a heart attack or something?"

"He's rich. Rich people don't have heart attacks."

Jordan glanced around the bathroom. The toilet seat was too heavy. The toothbrush holder was gold-plated. It went into the bag, along with a couple of ivory-handled brushes. There was nothing of much value under the sink, except some Wet Wipes; Jordan tossed them in the bag. He had run out the other day.

The third room proved to be some sort of art studio. An easel stood in the center of the room, where the light from two picture windows illuminated the surface of the portrait the doctor had been working on. The walls were bare. Next to the easel was a stool containing a palette and various brushes. In the corner between the two windows was another stool, this one supporting a small radio. There was no other furniture in the room.

"He paints?" Casey asked, walking around the easel so he could view what was on it.

"I guess so. Takes pictures *and* paints. I'd say he was gay, if it weren't for all the women in those photos."

"Painting isn't gay. Some of the greatest men in history painted." There was a pause. "I don't get it."

"How so many great men in history could be gay?"

"No. *This*."

Jordan walked over to his friend and stared at the portrait. It featured a

80

young woman, naked, her mouth smeared across her face as though in a grimace or some strange contortion. Behind her were flames; the woman was pale, almost white, and the background was orange and yellow and black. Her mouth was bright red.

"He hasn't finished her eyes yet?"

Her eyes were white, bare canvas.

Jordan shrugged. "Guess not. She had blond hair; probably had blue eyes. We should finish it for him."

"I don't want to touch it."

"You're right. It could be worth something."

"No. I mean, I want to leave it alone. I don't like it."

"You a fucking art critic now?"

"Let's just see what's in the other room, okay?"

Jordan's gazed shifted from Casey to the portrait. It would be a shame, to leave it. It was, in many ways, beautiful. Not conventionally, of course; no one would dare hang this painting above their mantelpiece. But Jordan thought, perhaps, that he could keep it in his closet. He could pull it out every now and then to look at and admire. Maybe sell it, one day. Maybe.

"Come on." Casey tugged at the sleeve of his t-shirt. Jordan shook his head, mumbled something monosyllabic and insulting, and they went back out into the hall. The door had been closed; they left it open.

The final room was an old-fashioned study—there was a giant mahogany

desk at the far end of the room, and the walls were lined with books. A globe stood in one corner, a hat rack in another. In front of the desk were two leather chairs; Jordan immediately crossed the room and sat down in one. He opened a cigar box on the desk and took one out.

"Wish I had a lighter."

"Are those Cuban?"

Jordan ignored the question. He put the cigar back and stood.

"Nice room. Look for a safe."

There was no safe.

Jordan placed the cigar box in the bag. He also grabbed from the desk an assortment of pens. There was a small golden clock, resting on a bookshelf, that also went into the bag.

"Bag's getting heavy," Jordan said, and handed it to Casey.

He took another look around the room before leaving. The walls were bare—wood paneling, maybe even real wood. But no pictures. No paintings. Seemed odd, a man who took so much delight in the visual arts not decorating much.

"Guess we go upstairs now," Jordan said. They went back into the hallway.

"I think we should go. I'm getting thirsty."

"What?"

"I said we should—"

"Hey, dipshit, I'm right here. I heard you. I *meant*, why the fuck should we leave? I saw a fridge in that kitchen."

"Yeah, but..."

Jordan waited. Casey's voice died out.

"Yeah. All right. Let's go to the kitchen and get you something to drink. *Then* we'll head upstairs."

As they went back into the kitchen, Jordan glanced at the front picture window again. Not much had changed out there; a few of the shadows had grown longer, perhaps, but nothing drastic. At least there wasn't a car in the driveway.

Casey went straight to the refrigerator. Jordan fumbled through the doctor's mail again, picking up envelopes and tossing them aside.

"Credit card bills...that Publisher's Clearinghouse kills me, I swear to god. *Entertainment Weekly*? Jesus."

Bottles rattled as Casey opened the refrigerator door.

"Bills. I wonder how much the doc owes. I bet it's nothing for him. You spend enough money impressing all those ladies, you got enough money to pay for electricity, you know?"

He listened to the low hum of the air conditioner as he picked up another envelope.

"There's nothing personal here. Goddammit, I'm bored. Tinkles, what's he got in there? Anything good?"

Casey didn't respond.

Jordan glanced back over his shoulder. Casey stood in front of the open fridge, one hand clutching the top of the door, the other hanging by his side. He stared into the fridge. The sunlight, coming through the window to his left, reflected off his glasses, causing a brief flare that made Jordan wince and shift his eyes.

"Hey, Tinkles, make up your fucking mind already."

Casey didn't budge.

"Tinkles? You're letting all the cold air out."

Casey's left hand, clutching the refrigerator door, shook.

"Tinkles?"

Jordan set down the mail and walked over to his friend. He glanced at Casey's face, followed his gaze, and stared into the fridge.

The two men stood there.

Jordan blinked, bit his lip, and blinked again. He coughed.

"It's a head."

Casey didn't react. His hand shook the door slightly, causing a rattle that made Jordan glance over his shoulder, afraid that someone would hear.

"No one's there," he said.

Casey didn't respond.

Jordan turned back to the fridge. "It's a head," he said again. "A fucking head."

She was young, roughly their age, with short blond hair and lips that had probably been full, but were now rough and blue. The worst part, the part that Jordan was sure kept Casey frozen in place, was that her eyes were open, and they still seemed alive.

Ridiculous; a head couldn't live without its body. But, yeah, that's what she looked like: a living head, cold but alive.

"Hey," he said.

She kept looking at him.

"What's the matter?" He leaned forward. "Come on, honey. Say something."

"Jordan."

Jordan jumped back out of the fridge, belatedly recognizing Casey's voice. He turned on his friend and slugged him in the shoulder.

"Jesus, Tinkles! I swear to Christ, man…"

"Jordan."

"Yeah, Tinkles?"

"It's a head."

"Yeah, Tinkles. A head."

"Jordan…"

"You got something to say, Tinkles, you say it."

Casey looked at him. Then back at the head in the fridge. "Who is she?"

Jordan stepped forward again, staring at the head. "If I had to guess, I'd say it's one of the girls from those photos. Hell, it could even be the chick in the painting. Hard to say, though; this gal's rather blue." He laughed.

"Lets get out of here."

Jordan didn't move. "Looks like our doctor has some…uh…*extracurricular* activities that he doesn't want people to know about it." He glanced at the picture window in the front room. "Odd, though, that he'd keep her *here*. I mean…there's *food* in there! Yuck."

Casey stepped toward the door that led to the garage. "Jordan, come on, let's get out of here."

"I wonder if *she's* in any of that Tupperware. You know? Like, does he *eat* them?"

Jordan couldn't tell if he was sickened by the thought. Probably.

"Jesus, Tinkles…this guy is *wicked*. Look at her neck, too…such a clean cut. I bet he used one of his scalpels, you know? He's a surgeon, after all. He's good with knives. I wonder where the rest of her is."

"Jordan, let's *go*."

"I ever tell you you're a pussy, Tinkles?"

Casey grabbed his shoulder. "Jordan, Goddammit! There's a fucking head in the fucking refrigerator!"

Jordan shook the hand off. "No shit. What you think I've been staring at the past five minutes, a jar of mayonnaise?"

Casey stared at him, then took a step back. "What's wrong with you?"

"There's nothing wrong with me, Tinkles, except the fact that there's still a lot of shit we have to grab. We ain't found his safe yet. It's probably upstairs."

"You…you still want to *rob* him?"

84

"He's rich, Tinkles."

"He's a psychopath!"

"He's still rich. Besides, he'll never know it was us."

"No." Casey raised his hands, stepping away. He pointed at the fridge. "That's a *head*, Jordan. And that painting. And

all those pictures. He's *crazy*, and we need to get the hell out of here and call the cops."

"The cops?" Jordan laughed. "Listen to yourself."

"An anonymous phone call, then."

"Tinkles. Look at me."

Casey turned his eyes away from the refrigerator. Jordan held his gaze a moment, then smiled.

"Tinkles, what do you think is gonna happen if we rob him? Huh? You know what'll happen? Nothing. He'll never call the cops; if he's got a chick's head in his *fridge*, think what he has stashed away elsewhere. I mean, the darkroom where he developed all those photographs…think of what's in *there*."

"I am, Jordan. That's *exactly* what I'm thinking about."

"If we call the cops, they'll come here. And you know what? They may find some evidence that we were robbing the place. Something that ties *us* into it. And maybe we could do some kinda plea, 'cause we called the cops, but probably not, because the system don't give a rats ass about you or me. Hell, they may deal with us worse than they do the doctor—he's *one* of them, a rich asshole. But that won't happen if we just leave. The cops will never come, and we won't get dragged into it."

Casey looked at him, then beyond his shoulder, out the front window. His thin frame shook, and his eyes moved restlessly.

"No cops, Casey. We get what we want, he gets what he wants. And hey—he'll probably screw up sometime. They always do."

"Okay." Casey looked at him. "Okay. Then let's leave. Now."

"Now? Hell no. We gotta see what else there is."

"I'm leaving, Jordan."

There was a firmness in his voice that caught Jordan off guard. He watched his friend closely, saw the stiffness of his cheeks and the resolve in his eyes. Jordan started to say something, but then he closed his mouth. He found himself nodding.

"All right. Okay." He swallowed down the bile that rose in his throat at the thought of leaving the house. "We'll go. Now."

"Okay." Casey made for the door to the garage.

Jordan watched him, then glanced back into the fridge. Such possibilities in the house. He shook his head as he closed the refrigerator door. Bottles rattled against each other. He held the girl's eyes, wondering what he'd do if she winked at him.

Probably piss himself.

"Tinkles. Wait up."

Casey was already through the garage and in the backyard, the duffel bag hanging limply in his grasp. Jordan followed him as slowly as he could. As he stepped out into the backyard, he took one last glance behind him. He saw a door he hadn't noticed earlier; it was along the rear wall of the garage, and low to the ground, like a storm cellar.

That's where the darkroom is.

The darkroom…and other things. He almost told Casey to stop. They hadn't bothered to check the upstairs; they should at least check the cellar, while they were here.

"Jordan, *come on.* Hurry the fuck up."

Casey was at the fence, waiting to give Jordan a boost up. His head kept moving—left-to-right, right-to-left, up and down. Looking for witnesses. Or the doctor.

Jordan backed out of the doorway with a soft cough. It had meant to come out as a sigh, but his throat was too dry. He blinked in the sunlight, the darkness of the garage and the house still in his head as he crossed the yard to his friend. The whole way, he kept glancing over his shoulder, thinking of the worn paneling on the door, the rusted handle. A damn shame.

The things rich doctors keep in their basements…

Dan Davis was born and raised in Central Illinois.
His work has appeared in various online and print journals.

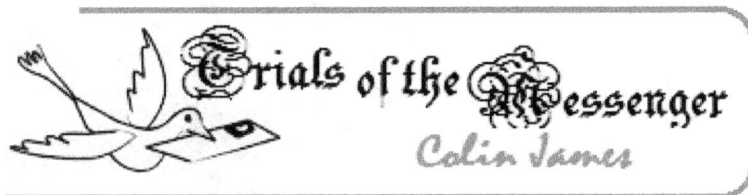

Trials of the Messenger
Colin James

If you follow the canyon trail down,
the blunderbusses will pick you off
from up on the high ridge.
There is absolutely no cover
save for a few pomegranate bushes.
these having been picked over by the birds,
your faces visible through the branches.
So what if the pragmatic blasts
won't reach across the divide,
You're connected to your apprehension.
The litter you've collected won't save you.

Colin James works in Energy Conservation.
He is a great admirer of the Scottish landscape painter, John Mackenzie.

The Man Who Fell Out Of His Head

Evander Arnage

The night Lewis Lipitt was struck by a bolt of lightening he was retrieving a string of socks he'd left hanging outside his four story kitchen window that looked down on the small square courtyard of his brownstone apartment block. He had heard the thunder rolling in and felt the blue flickers of the lightening on his cheek while he was stooped over his bathroom sink trimming his chronically unkempt mustache and had recalled the socks just in the nick of time before the rain began to fall.

They were good white socks, the sort you could wear with anything, even a black suit despite the warnings in back pages of various men's style magazines to avoid doing just that, but Lewis didn't care. He liked his socks thick and white and washed in a good lather of fabric softener so that when he put them on this feet he could slide around on the hard wood floor like he was riding two little cloud cushions.

Just before the lightening hit he was thinking 'what fun it will be to glide around the apartment in a crashing thunder storm!'
He was reaching out with his gut leaning on the windowsill pulling a sock from a clothespin when it struck. There was no sound at all, at least not to his ears. He felt only a rush of air somewhere between his ears. He had no idea he had been hit by lightening, it was sudden and

inexplicable and all at once he felt as though he had become unglued from his own reality and was now somehow inside of the sock he had just been holding, not his body per say but his presence. His perspective was emanating out of it and he felt a great ocean of gray limbo-ness surrounding him. A terrible thought occurred to him then: 'what if this was really his reality? That he was, and had always been, this sock and what he had known up until now, his life as a man, his apartment his entire past- childhood, teenage years, college, jobs, travel, girlfriends, struggles and desires- had all been a long and vivid sock dream and that this was, and had always been, his one true reality, this particulate clump of white cotton fiber that had spontaneously developed awareness and then projected itself into the unconscious fantasy of 'Lewis the human being' but was now returned to its normal state of inconsequential molecules without free will or physical mobility or intelligent intent.

Lewis was clenched by a deep belief in this, it was so clear and true and immediately he felt a powerful anguish for the loss of the dream life he once lived, as Lewis Lippit the struggling composer and failed lover, who measured his worth by all the things he had never done but wanted to and stayed up late at night doing anything to avoid going to bed just so he wouldn't have to be alone with own his bitter judgments. Then with nothing else to do for it he accepted the futility of lamenting what had never really been anyway and made peace with his new state, his one true reality, realizing as he did how simple and serene a reality it was. To not have the worries of the human body as it aged and the human experiences as they multiplied and became more convoluted, the interminable labors for money, relationships, status, possessions, the fear of pain, injury, mortality. He would need none of those now, he was simply an inanimate piece of the physical landscape and could satisfy himself with the essential imperative to be- and that was all.

A great, euphoric tide washed over him like he had never known, a deep satisfaction with the simplicity of his own presence. So fulfilling was it that he no longer even felt the need to identify himself as himself, or as an individual entity at all. He was simply matter-awareness. There was no more need for an ego, the burden of purpose had been lifted from him and he now floated in a serenity of blissful ubiquity. He was sock.

Lewis was allowed to enjoy this profound experience for only a brief moment though before he was violently sucked out of the sock perspective and came to in a coughing, sputtering fit, back inside his body which felt stiff and smelled of burnt hair. He could hear light jazz music playing on the radio in the living room and the sound of the rain pattering against the window above his head. The sock was still clutched tightly in his fist and smoke emanated from a black scorch mark in the sole. Later he would wrap it in a silk handkerchief and save it in the bottom of his dresser where he would take it out sometimes on anxious nights and yearn for its uncomplicated existence before satisfying himself with the thought that in the end there would only be transition.

Evan is a freelance copywriter and creative consultant from Toronto currently working on his first book, an illustrated collection of fantastically absurd short stories entitled *The Human Fable.* When not writing Evan provides a devastating percussion element to the musical triumvirate *La Mini Band* in his adopted city of Buenos Aires.

Issue 4 Photography by Courtney Lantz

According to Courtney: *I think a general theme for the philosophy behind my photography would be a discovery of the complexity and intrigue in simple, mundane things most people look at every day, but rarely actually see. I don't, however, consider myself a niche photographer. While I typically try to focus on geometric patterns that would make for an interesting macro, I'm not immune to taking a photo of something like a sunset or lightning, just because it's pretty. I really enjoy the challenge of trying to turn something into a mystery, trying to disguise something most people would recognize fairly easily as something abstract or unidentifiable.*

Courtney was born in Reno, NV and has lived all over the US since. She currently resides in Louisville, KY with her boyfriend Tom and two ball pythons Pericles and Zeno.

90

At The Crossroads

Pat Hebert

The note read, "You have something of mine, and I want it back." The notepaper still holds a trace of his body heat and it amuses me that he left the note himself. I can't help but unfold the note again and re-read its contents. Reading it isn't easy mind you because the spelling is atrocious but this is not the first time I've received this type of note.

I enjoy my occasional trips to Mississippi and the fascinating people I meet while I'm there. What tickles me to no end is how frequently I'm invited in this supposed pious God fearing place. It's almost as frequent as I'm invited to Nashville Tennessee, the buckle of the Bible belt. But no matter, life and business goes on and we all have a role to fill in this grand play we call life.

But Robert's note has the unmistakable charm of those who want out now that my part of the bargain has been fulfilled. Short and sweet and right to the point as all the notes are but I wonder why he didn't wait for me to arrive? He went to all the trouble of summoning me which required he travel to Dockery Plantation and perform the ritual again. He had the courage to do it before and ask for my desperately needed help but now he's a coward? How unbecoming and tacky.

I am less than amused because it's August in Mississippi and it's hot. Usually I have no way of knowing who is summoning me so I take great care to dress appropriately in a gentlemanly fashion. I don't want to scare people unnecessarily because they're already nervous. Today I've dressed in a fine summer weight beige linen suit but as soon as I arrive, the heat is causing my shirt to cling to my back like a mud clings to a pig. Writer's have it so wrong when they state Hell is hot. It's not. It's a very comfortable temperature with consistent weather year round. Sort of like Hawaii without the rainy season. I take great care in my appearance and I don't want it marred by perspiration created in an unpleasant environment.

But back to my friend Robert, his charming little note and the effort required to obtain my attention. I have a memory like no other so when I heard the voice calling, I knew it was my friend Robert immediately. I was so pleased to hear from him again and am hopeful that he brought his guitar. I do love to hear him play.

"Robert! Robert Johnson! I'm here and have received your note. We must talk."

One of the aspects of the agreement that is so convenient is if I need to call for one of my little lambs all I need to do is speak in my regular speaking voice and they'll hear me no matter where they're located. With that done, I now wait for Robert to gather the courage and show himself. I hope he remembers how much I hate to wait. I am extremely busy.

Surveying the area, there's a small patch of bushes on the side of the road but nothing else. I really must find more convenient area to conduct these meetings. There's nowhere to sit or purchase a cool drink. But therein lies the problem. No one wants to be in the middle of a bustling town performing the summoning ritual. They do look a little ridiculous as they do it but that's part of the design. I got quite tired of farm boys asking for the hand of some noblemen's comely daughter when their pants were on fire. So it's a bit of work for them. I regret that I'm never able to witness it firsthand but my minions have regaled me with stories that do keep me amused.

Sweat is now beginning to bead along my hatband and this is a new hat. My friend Robert truly is beginning to try my patience. Perhaps he needs to be taught the consequences of incurring my displeasure.

"Robert. You called me. I'm here, and I've read your note so clearly we must talk. Please show yourself so we can put this tiresome business behind us and we can find a place for a whiskey. I know you enjoy a whiskey from time to time."

What seems like a interminably long wait, the bushes begin to move and I am relieved that this foolishness is about to come to it's logical conclusion. It's almost laughable for one of these little flesh bags to think I don't know what is meant by the note and it's ominous 'I want it back'.

Darting out from the bushes however, is a mangy stray dog who stops dead in the middle of the road and turns it's beady eyes to me. With a wag of it's tail, it begins trotting towards me with a surprising sense of purpose. I know this is not Robert so what is going on here? The mutt reaches me, sits directly in front of me and looks up at me beseechingly. Glancing around I'm beginning to expect my old boss has sent one or more of his crew and the dog is a distraction. But there's no one but me and this dog.

"Hello there you bag of bones. Where did you come from?"

The heat must be getting to me because I actually spoke to this creature. I am truly annoyed now. I was in the middle of breaking in a new associate when Robert called. I was just getting to one of my favorite parts. I love when a newly arrived little lamb realizes I do collect the debt they owe me. It's at that moment they realize  they've asked for too little and should have been a little greedy. However, my favorite, favorite moment is right after they've learned what's in store for them and they beg for a way out. The look of sheer terror on their faces is priceless. Were they not paying attention in Sunday school? I guess not. But back to my favorite moment of all. It's that wonderful moment when I tell them getting out of the agreement was available to them at all times. Of course, before they died. All they had to do is return to My Father. How easy. All they had to do is accept His Son as their savior. Anyone could manage that don't you think? I do thank my Father daily about how stupid he made these flesh bags. They're completely asinine. My dear Robert has now blackened my mood and I am quite tired of waiting.

"Robert. You need to meet me now. I am on my last nerve."

No movement anywhere. Crumpling the note, I toss it back to the center of the crossroads and it begins to smolder and then catches flame. With the summons answered, I've fulfilled my part of the bargain, yet again.

Just as I'm about back to my place, unbelievably, I am summoned again. Can you believe it? Twice in one day? It's not Robert much to my disappointment but what is wrong with these people? Can't they do anything for themselves?

I take my time in responding because due to the heat, I need a change of wardrobe. I've changed from the linen suit into a charming blue and white seersucker. More lightweight than linen, I'm truly hopeful that this will stand up to the heat.

Arriving back at the crossroads, I'm surprised by who I see. It is truly unusual but it's a woman. Not really a woman, but a young girl on the cusp of womanhood who looks absolutely stricken with terror. But underneath it, I can tell she's truly heartbroken.

"Well my lamb. What seems to be the trouble?" She just about jumps out of her skin when I speak to her. She stands in the middle of the crossroads, mouth agape, she clutches the top of her dress to her chest.

"Who are you?" she asks in a voice that's low and husky as her eyes dart around.

"Who do you think I am?" I answer. This is beginning to get fun.

"I don't know."

"Why are you here in the middle of the night? It's not safe for a sweet young woman such as yourself to be out alone." I love ratcheting up the fear just a tad.

"I was told if I came here, I could get what I want."

Oh my. This one is challenged considering none of them are all that swift in the brains department. But who can blame me for having some fun. After all, Robert completely ruined my evening. So I ask, "Isn't this the place you can come and the Devil will give you everything you ask for?"

"Yeah."

"Is he here yet?"

"I dunno. What he look like?"

"Doesn't he have horns?"

"I dunno. He ain't looking like no fancy boy like you though."

Fancy boy? Is that a good thing I wonder?

"Maybe I'm the Devil." Well I shouldn't have said that. The little lamb has now urinated all over herself. That's just unhygienic.

"Oh lamb. Don't worry. Nothing bad is going to happen. Yes, I am indeed the one you want to talk to. But I'm completely harmless now aren't I?"

"Thought you'd be red with horns and hooves and stuff."

"Oh dear. That's just a writer with no imagination. Or should I say too much imagination. I'm perfectly normal as you can see. How can I help you?"

"I dunno. I think I should go."

Buyers remorse already. My my. I'll need to work fast with this one.

"I can see you're sad. Has someone broken your heart?"

A shake of the head in the affirmative but the eyes are just about to pop out of her head as she stares at me.

"Now darling, don't be frightened. I mean you no harm and I'm here to help you. How brave of you to take charge of your life and do what you need to do to make things happen."

"Yeah! That's what I tell Sadie and she just said I be crazy. But I knows you can help. I went to the lady at the carnival and what she gave me did nothing. Took my money and Pa finded out and whipped me."

"Oh, how awful. Is it your father you need my help with?"

"No!"

Shuffling feet has started to kick up dust that is floating perilously close to my new clean suit. These flesh bags, so dumb and careless.

"Sweetheart. Why don't you tell me your name. Once we're on a first name basis, this will be just like two old friends talking."

"Maebelle."

"Oh how pretty. Maebelle what?" The first step is for them to give you their full name. That begins the connection and once you have that, extracting the agreement is just a few small steps away.

"Maebelle Vesta Charlton."

"Maebelle Vesta Charlton, I'm glad to make your acquaintance. I'm Lucifer. But call me Lucy, all my friends do."

"Lucy? Are you joking me? The Devil goes by Lucy?"

Well I'll be damned, the stupid little thing begins to giggle. But then I see the brilliance in all of it, she's no longer scared. I can wrap this up in no time and be home in time for this evening's ritual impaling.

"Why stand on formality. Now tell me, I'm guessing you need a love potion."

"Yes!"

"First Maebelle, tell me a little about him so I know exactly what you need. By the way, how old are you?"

"I'm 19. He's a guitar player that stayed with us and he was my boyfriend until he went away."

Oh do my ears deceive me? This evening may not be a waste after all.

"A musician? There's just something about a musician isn't there. Tell me his name."

"Robert. Robert Johnson."

I'm giddy. I would do a little jig but I mustn't be too eager.

"What happened?"

"He left to go play some juke joint and he ain't been back. I love him and I think I have his baby."

"Oh my. You're father will not be happy about that. We must get him back where he belongs, don't we?"

"Yes! See I knew you'd help me."

"Maebelle, are you willing to do exactly as I ask you to? No questions asked if I promise you that Robert with be with you always?"

"Yes! I'll do anything!"

See, it's just so easy.

"Excellent. First, you'll need to travel to Greenwood Mississippi which isn't to far from here. Go to the juke joint…"

"I can't go there! Decent women don't go there."

"No, no, darling. You won't go there at night. You'll go there during the day and ask for Robert. Tell them who you are and where you're staying. I promise you Robert will come visit."

"Okay. What then? I tell him I love him?"

"You tell him that if you want to scare him away! No, you don't say anything other than sweet things."

"I can do that. But how I make him stay?"

"After you go to the juke joint, I need you to be very brave again. Can you do that?"

"Yeah. But what I got to do?"

"Can you get some whiskey?"

"My daddy make it."

"Excellent. Bring a bottle of whiskey with you and make sure you have it ready for Robert. But we're going to put a love potion in it first."

"You give me that right?"

"Silly girl. Go to the hardware store in Greenwood and tell the owner that Lucy sent you. He'll give you the potion, don't let him talk you out of it, then you'll say the words I'll give you over it. You then mix the love potion into the whiskey and make sure Robert drinks all of it. From that moment on, Robert will be with you forever."

The idiot is now grinning ear to ear and it looks like she's about to rush toward me and hug me.

"I'm gonna send all my girlfriens here! Thank you Lucy I knowed you help me!"

At that statement, I'm a little nauseous thinking that my companions for eternity will be these love sick girls.

"You run along, lamb. After Robert drinks all the love potion, tell him that Lucy said hello."

Pat Hebert is a Nashville based writer/musician who doesn't miss New England winters. When she's not writing or playing guitar, she enjoys yoga, movies, cooking and maintaining a sense of humor.

Knight Of Despair

N. A'Yara Stein

Jesus and Judas were best friends.

A bear chained to nothing more than himself,
Judas thinks he should have been more like his brother
who worked in the daytime and got paid a salary,
instead of in drugs and jewelry and tips.

Subject to fits of disorganized boredom, he scratches himself
in the longest night. He lies alone, in the pale light,
180 pounds of mere matter all heartbreak and ridiculous.

By turns feckless and reckless,
his attempts to be helpful create no end of trouble;
pitied art thou among snitches.

He claims what happened that April night was simple.
An empty ritual repeated with each piece of silver counted out –

almost like a dream, illogically logical, shockingly normal.

But in this certain kind of light, this certain kind
that follows him around now all the time,
he keeps hearing the silence inside his own heart.
And, of course, he can't sleep.

Out among the chorfing, anonymous throng
he laughs like daybreak without fear of midnight,
indulges in and mocks his own suspicions.
So little time to live a life in this desert.

Later he celebrates, drinks and laughs at Maisel's;
like a sultan, she adorns the walls with floating smoke.
He sniffs the fire, goes down to the cellar for fig preserves.

He is a smooth operator and he lied before,
but he wants her to know that *today*
every tiny thing glitters in the shiver of his tears.

N. A'Yara Stein is a Romani-American poet and writer living on a chicory farm and has been nominated twice for the 2010 Pushcart Prize. She holds an MFA from the University of Arkansas and is a grant recipient of the Michigan Art Council and the Arkansas Arts Council. The former editor of the arts quarterly Gypsy Blood Review, she's recently published in Verse Wisconsin, The Birmingham Arts Journal, The Chaffey Review, The San Pedro Poetry Review , The Delinquent, UK, among others. She lives near Chicago with her sons, is looking for a book publisher, and is the featured poet in the next issue of The James Dickey Review.

An Old Man
George Spain

A summer evening.

The hot, dry air has not yet begun to cool.

The sky is gray-blue and cloudless

Across the sky hundreds of turkey buzzards glide on the rising heat waves, heading southward to their roosts in the pine mountains. Far below them a man is sitting alone on a narrow ledge atop a red, sandstone mesa. He is an old man. He is watching the sunset.

The mesa's steep cliffs rise high above a barren plain that stretches far off in every direction. To the west the plain ends in a dark range of hills. Just above the hills the sun is a brilliant orange.

The man closes his eyes and prays silently and slowly–

'Sun Father hear my prayer.
My spirit is filled with pain.
Night Bird's small breath is gone.
She will not laugh again.
My people are almost gone.
Our animals have all died.
The corn and grass have no life.
Our land is dry and broken.
The rains do not come.
The springs have turned to sand.
Father hear my prayer, send clouds filled with water.'

He prays three times then opens his eyes, raises his head and looks at the sky. There are no clouds. The birds are gone. The sun almost gone. All across the horizon the sky is bright red. He does not move. He is sitting cross-legged with his hands on his knees, his body still as the stone slab that he sits upon. The stone is smooth and long.

The old man is small and shrunken by age and starvation. He is dressed in a calico shirt, loose cotton pants and deerskin moccasins; they are tattered and gray with dirt and ashes. His skin is the color of mahogany. His coal-black hair is streaked gray and cut short in bangs above his deep-set eyes; it hangs in long, straight locks on the sides and back of his head. A black head-band is tied around his head. The bones of his face are so sharp they seem barely covered by skin.

The skin is like the parched earth: covered in dust, every inch lined and cracked a thousand times. The lips of his widespread mouth are white and split. It is an old, weathered face, strained and exhausted by hunger and lack of sleep. But most of all by sadness. Only his son and grandson are still alive. His wife and all the others of his family have died. His thoughts are not clear. Since midday the past and present have mixed with things not real.

Now the sky is deep blue. The same blue as when he first came here, a little boy on his father's back, holding tight around his father's neck, as his father climbed the steep trail to the ledge.

He smells the sweet smell of burning sage and tobacco. The smell of his father. He feels his dead father with him now: his body beside him on the stone, touching his hand, whispering in his ear, telling him-- *'Look up.'*

He looks above his father. The air is so clean and clear the night's first stars seem to almost touch his head. They seem so near he thinks he could pull them from the dark. He feels his father's rough hand on his and his soft breath on his cheek as he tells him the old stories. Tells them in his low, singsong voice--

'Never forget all of this. All you see around you was created before my grandfather's grandfathers, long before the ancient ones came here, before the days of light when Sky Father came down to Earth Mother. These stories are how all things came to be. Remember them and when you are grown tell them to our people. Tell them these things–

When Sky Father came down to the great caves in the mountains he entered Mother Earth and together they gave us all of life that is in us and around us. First, they created all the things that do not move and the things that grow from the earth, and then all of the beings that

breathe–these came from the caves: walking, crawling, flying, and those that swim came swimming in the waters. And with all of these creatures came those that walk two-legged–those who became the first people. All of these that came from the caves brought seeds of corn and beans and grass and the nuts for every kind of tree to grow in Earth Mother.

When all of this was done Sky Father poured his waters upon Earth Mother so that all things could be green and filled with life. But Sky Father saw that nothing could grow or find it's way without light. So he reached deep into the earth and scooped fire up into his hands and rolled it around and around until it became a ball which we call Sun Father. He placed it in the dark where it would give light for the time that he called day. And then he let it turn it's face away for sleep and for rest, the time he called night.

Then Sky Father saw there were creatures who flew and walked by night, and that they needed small lights to see their way. So he reached again into the earth and, this time, took handfuls of coals into his palms and flung them across the darkness...'

His father's voice fades, the sweet odor and the touch of his hand are gone. He looks to his side--turns-- and looks behind himself.

He is alone.

He looks down at his hands. They are veined and splotched, the fingers twisted–the small one on his left hand is missing–the knuckles and wrists are gnarled. He touches his hands, holds them up close to his face, turns them over, examines them, then places them palms down on his knees.

"Huh. Look my father, I have grown old. Soon I will come to be with you, but first I must see my son. I do not know where he is."

He listens but hears nothing. He tries to shout but his dry throat and mouth can only rasp–"Where are you my son? My legs are weak. I do not know where I am. Come take me on your back from this place."

There is no answer.

The sun has dropped below the horizon. The last soft rays of light are red and orange and gold. The old man closes his eyes and prays–

'You my Fathers hear me! My people die.

Send your wind-blown clouds,
Send your blue-black clouds,
Send your tall clouds filled with waters.
Bring them with their ladders of lightning,
Bring them with their roaring sounds of thunder,
Bring them with their many rivers of waters.
Nourish Earth Mother with the life of your living waters,
Nourish the burned corn plants and all seeds with your living waters,
Nourish my people and the creatures of all kind with your living waters.

This I pray.'

His head lowers. His eyes blink open, then close. His shoulders slump. His breathing is shallow and jagged. He sleeps...

And she is there. Night Bird stands before him: laughing, calling his name, reaching up to him...

He jerks awake.

The ledge is shaking. Sounds are coming from the stones and the air beyond the ledge: roaring, howling, bells and drums growing louder and louder until they are directly in front of him. And he sees them--

Before him there are tall shapes dancing upright in the air. Half human–half animal: bears, coyotes, pumas, eagles and deer. Their bodies are painted with bright green, yellow, white, red, blue and black spots and zig-zags. They are chanting and growling, beating drums and rattling gourds; some are carrying plumed prayer-sticks, others bows and arrows; they shuffle forward almost touching the ledge; he smells their animal smells, hears them grunting deep in their throats as they lift their knees high, then stomp downward into the dark, twisting and turning back and forth so near he sees himself reflecting in their eyes. He is dancing with them in the air: half man-half wolf, howling over and over, with war-clubs in each hand. He feels the dancer's movements and heat and the vibrations of the stone and music. His lungs fill with air. His legs are swift and strong.

All this flashes before him for an instant and then...

They are gone. He is there alone on the ledge. Far out on the plains wolves and coyotes howl before they begin their nightly hunt.

The air is cool.

Not far down the cliff there is a quick clatter of rocks.

A child laughs.

The old man tries to stand but cannot. A great tiredness comes over him. He cannot feel his feet and legs or lift his hands. He wants to call a name but the thought leaves him. His head bends forward. His breath flows out without a sound. His lips and eyelids open slightly. Slowly his body leans over sideways onto the stone slab.

Stars light the ledge.

Rocks clatter just beneath.

George Spain--native Tennessean, retired mental health worker with a family so large and colorful it includes one of everything.

The Silenced

DOA Worrell

    The wind pushed south, in phases and infrequent like a stuttering breeze, and gradually dwindling with the horizon's narrowing light. But seated in a thick patch of bushes on the steep hillside Dae-Ho couldn't feel a thing. His gaze entangled in the thorny shrubs and high meadow grass that thrashed back in the breeze and the fall shaded trees whipping to the side as if tossing their hair. He also noticed his own camouflaged jacket incessantly swell with wind then gradually shrink like the croak of a mute toad. Dae-Ho could see the wind clearly as an emerald ocean splashing and whirling around him but couldn't feel it, because sometimes when he stared too closely it made him numb.

    They coined this the "anesthetic sense" in the North Korean army, a term originating from winter snipers in the early sixties. Their entire bodies hibernated for hours in the snow drenched hills of Kaesong with only the whites of their eyes astir. It was a state that few North Korean soldiers could achieve and Dae-Ho Jung was one of them. Though from today onward, sitting silent while countless others prayed the evening's national anthem, he wasn't one of them anymore.

    Dae-Ho sat in a thicket of bushes just a few meters east of the dirt road he trailed the night before. The bushes were dense, giving him just enough visibility to keep an eye on the jeeps and other military vehicles that routinely swept the restricted streets and dirt paths.

    His camouflage was a couple shades off the viridian-hued bushes around him but close enough that it wasn't conspicuous. Though he knew the black semiautomatic rifle around his shoulder with its silver clip and the sable shaded silencer on his waist were in a word, eye-catching. *Two words*, Dae-Ho then thought, though he figured he had two guns and that was one word each.

    Dae-Ho's thoughts slipped in and out of focus. The envelope in his breast pocket and the border a few miles off on the horizon brought thoughts of South Korea, his fiancée, or the thousand other daydreams that might branch off. Though somehow these notions would always reunite on one thought: death, and Dae-Ho would immediately regain his focus, clutching his rifle, surveying the vista and letting everything else recede.

    The only moment Dae-Ho let the poise slip from his trigger finger was when he tapped his chest so that the envelope with cash, photographs and other documents inside rustled like a paper heartbeat.

He knew it was there. He had touched the materials just a few minutes earlier but needed to check it again to calm his constant nerves. This envelope with documents and photos of North Korean atrocities had turned into a pressure point while his finger became the needle of acupuncture. As light as it was, the envelope made a far heavier burden than the guns or bulky camouflage and body armor strapped to his chest. Of all the secrets Dae-Ho kept in his heart, the gravest one now lay next to it.

He never believed he'd end up here. Here, somewhere between Kaesong and the South Korean border. A border that he once guarded like a jealous husband, Dae-Ho was now trying to cross himself. Sometimes he felt he committed some infidelity of ego and the irony almost made him smile but didn't. His cheeks didn't quite rise high enough, the single dimple on his left cheek didn't quite fall in deep enough, and his expression lingered between a smirk and nothing at all. He just couldn't seem to completely smile anymore since his fiancée died about six months earlier. *Had it been that long?* He began to think; then he tried not to.

His face had become the same as the peasant farmers or the occasional local pedestrian he sometimes passed on the passenger side window of whatever military van or truck he rode in. Their barren expressions seemed so unmistakable even as he sped by. Their eyes would hook and swing dance like a Doppler for the eyes. But in that moment or less Dae-Ho could see a face narrowed into an expression that hadn't seemed to change in years, and it wasn't until now that he understood why.

The forest green fatigues with ruffles on the shoulders and matching hat with a rim that always lined his eyes with an ominous shadow drew the line between him and the average North Korean citizen. He felt it immediately, this peeling sensation then the eventual separation, during his daily marches along the near empty streets in uniform.

He always heard silence throttled to the very last breath as he strolled by the swarms of loiterers around makeshift markets and food stands. Smiles and nods even the occasional salute would skip from person to person in the most unnatural way. It wasn't a willing motion or even a reflex but almost seemed a sort of twitch. The type of twitch that crooks the neck when a prickling drizzles like raindrops down the spine. And as Dae-Ho would continue past them he always heard whispers burst out in exhaustion as if they had been holding back their words like their breath.

He couldn't remember what had caused it. Why he split from the common man like an asexual cell. Though he believes it might have been the propaganda that sounded so repetitive it began to echo through his mind, resounding between every thought, from *where did I put my keys* to *what should I have for lunch*. Eventually it became a quiet conscience in the back of his head that talked him out of empathy and cooled the burning sensation that stuck to his chest when he executed men for stealing for their families or glanced down at the desperation of the prostitutes underneath him.

The feeling remained, the love for his country and people, that sense hadn't left him and one could say it grew even stronger. Though thinking back on it now he feels the sense of love mixed and muddled into other senses and ideas like staring into a kiss or trying to touching a whisper. And from other's point of view it seemed that Dae-Ho ignored the suffering that spilled out from his rifle. As an executioner he put to death men and women by the hundreds and orphaned countless children. But in his logic, silencing one or two or more for the stability of millions saved the very children he orphaned.

It got to the point that the villagers began to pay Dae-Ho just to speak for them about residential problems, like the overflow of village sewage or the lack of proper irrigation for their crops. They feared so much to speak out about these issues that they would slip him a few chon or won merely to have him speak on their behalves. And even with the government always in his right ear and his propaganda conscience at the other, Dae-Ho couldn't help but feel guilty. *Of all things*, he would think, *speaking at least should be free.*

A twig snapped into the silence, then another and it took one more before Dae-Ho realized footsteps were approaching. The person's feet dawdled and stepped nearly inaudible as if they purposely slinked towards him and tiptoeing so quietly in fact that at times it sounded as if they barely touched the ground.

Did they know? He thought but wasted no time in lifting his rifle towards the tiny opening in the bushes that he crawled through twelve hours earlier. His instincts flinched into place. His hand and trigger finger remained steady, his breathing stayed measured and constant and his eyelids not once fell into a blink. In the army they trained soldiers like Dae-Ho to make the unnatural natural and Dae-Ho felt most natural now with the trigger as an extension of his fist and the scope an extension of his eyes.

The shadow came first, swallowing light already crooked and dimmed under the evening sun. Then the bushes shuddered and with it the rustle of half dead leaves and an array of shadows shifting Dae-Ho's features in and out of shade and light. Not a moment later stubby feet came into view, followed by a waist wrapped in diapers, until finally the head of a baby boy no older than eighteen months was revealed.

Dae-Ho's finger sprang from the trigger immediately and he lowered the rifle. He could see the boy clearer now with the scope gone and his squinted eyes opening. Russet smudges lined the undoubtedly hand-me-down cloth diapers with blue patterned flowers that had faded nearly completely into the white. One of the boy's hands lay on his little belly, also smudged in that reddish-brown hue, probably from the plowed potato fields in the villages to the north. His other hand dug into his nose lined with trails of snot that stopped at his upper lips.

Standing barely half a meter high the boy could see clearly into the low-slung cavity that Dae-Ho had crawled into and consequently turned to Dae-Ho. With a whimper and lack of hesitation the boy stepped under the thorny bushes with Dae-Ho in site like the light at the end of the tunnel.

"Go back," Dae-Ho whispered but his voice only seemed to lead the boys towards him. "Go back," Dae-Ho repeated, this time with a flap of his hand.

Yet the little boy continued towards Dae-Ho with his hands stretched at his sides as if mimicking an airplane. When in fact the uneven patches of soil and stones laid out in front of him drove the boy to flatten his arms onto the air as if holding on to invisible crutches.

Dae-Ho couldn't fathom how the boy got this far out. The nearest village was more than half a mile to the north. Even if the boy came from the farm at the edge of the village, which judging by his soiled hands and diapers he more than likely did, it would have taken his little feet more than half an hour to arrive at the edge of this civilian dirt road.

Dae-Ho figured the boy was the son of a prostitute. One of countless infants who ran wild outside as their mothers worked. Despite the fact that prostitution was illegal and punishable by death it remained the most common expense of government officials. No one spoke out about prostitutions rings that had girls abducted from homes and trained in the arts of satisfaction. And anyone who did speak out never spoke out again. This point in particular Dae-Ho had the most difficulty forgetting because his fiancée spoke out against this very thing.

"Go home," Dae Ho griped, trying not to even glance at the boy who stood barely a meter away from him, hoping somewhere in his imagination that if he ignored the boy long enough he'd simply go away.

Though as Dae-Ho's vision slipped into the corners of his eyes, he saw the boy staring at him with a reminiscent pout that brought to mind street beggars and stray dogs. The boy suffered from malnutrition and it appeared as obvious to Dae-Ho as the boy's bulging belly button, now pointing him directly in the face.

The boy began fussing in protest of his Dae-Ho's lack of attention. Somewhere mixed in his undeveloped pronunciation, limited vocabulary and Kaesong dialect, words struggled desperately to surface. One of which sounded

107

like *water*, though in his southern North Korean accent it almost resembled the word *door*.

But Dae-Ho didn't pay enough attention to hear details in the boy's accent. He was too busy hushing him, not simply with the flush of air between his teeth but with gestures and suggestive expressions that to his dismay only pushed the boy to fuss and fret louder and try even harder to squeeze the words between his infant lips. Then something did slip out. Amid the tumultuous exchange of swirls and slurs of his tongue. Dae-Ho heard the word, *no*.

It was reminiscent and more so a flashback for Dae-Ho. He felt as if he suddenly tripped over the boy's voice and fell hard into a memory from six months earlier. Their voices sounded the same, men and women, sobbing and pleading for their lives like children. Though unlike children their voices weren't muffled by infancy but by the bag draped around their heads.

Dae-Ho stood in front of them that night at the head of a firing squad. He never saw their faces and didn't know what crime they committed but he did what he had done each time he was asked to do something questionable. He didn't ask a question and instead listened to a propaganda conscience that whispered, *"pull the trigger."* And he did.

There was the crackle of bullets, screams, shrieks then someone said in a whispered that carried in the wind, *no*. All of which should have gone routine for Dae-Ho but something just felt wrong about that night's executions. Something besides the fact that with most other death sentences a reason was given to why they executed the prisoners. And it wasn't just the larger amount of women this time around or the voices of a few prisoners that sounded like adolescents. Something seeped into the air that night that even to a veteran executioner like Dae-Ho just felt wrong.

Dae-Ho remembered the ride home that night. The soldiers didn't exchange a word in the military SUV nor did they listen to the buzz of static clogging up the music on the aging radio. Every soldier who took part in the execution sat with their heads bowed and bobbling. The only noises were that of wrenching metal as they hooked tight around corners and the rubber pummeling the dirt roads as they bounced over unpaved shortcuts to get home.

They dropped Dae-Ho off in front of his house and he immediately began feeling lightheaded. All he thought about was changing out of his uniform and resting his face on his fiancée's supple chest. Though his fiancée never returned home that night. She had gotten abducted in a government raid earlier in the evening and then taken to an undisclosed location. A bag was put over her head, then she was shot, and shot to death.

His propaganda conscience had always told him that for the stability of the country voices had to be sacrificed. That silencing one or two to avoid riots or rebellion was the small price that had to be paid. And he himself never lied to his family about the goings-on inside the government's secret police or even to his fiancée about prostitutes. He found that the best way not to lie is not too say anything at all.

Secret service soldiers like Dae-Ho were encouraged and an implication off of coerced to keep quiet about the executions. They took an oath of silence with their hands over their chests and the almighty flag waving above them. But after perhaps killing his own fiancée a bitter aftertaste lingered on his tongue every time he saluted or sang the national anthem. An excess of profanity came to mind each time and for him it felt a bit like swallowing his own vomit. Then he realized he couldn't silence himself anymore. It was all going to come spewing out and Dae-Ho knew he needed to reach that border or else anything he had to say would fall on deaf ears.

The skid of tires, as sudden as it was sharp, screeched from the side of the road and ground the gravel and pebbles into crackles and pops. Dae-Ho whipped forward as if he sat in the vehicle that came to a sudden stop at the side of the road. He lunged for the boy, grabbing his tiny hand and dragging his seemingly weightless body towards him. Though the boy's stubby bare feet couldn't keep up. He tripped, skidding his knees and stumping his toe against the litter of stones, snapped twigs and their protruding thorns, threatening with sharpness.

The boy stared at the thirty year old soldier through a screen tears. His lips shuddered like bubbles from the spout of a kettle rearing to burst into noise. Then the whimpering started, short and sudden breathing like an engine that wouldn't start, beginning with a breath and ended with a sniffle.

Dae-Ho panicked and reached blindly for his rifle. His gaze in the meantime weaved between the leaves and snapped stems and tried to procure an accurate headcount of the men in the back of the truck. His head nodded each time he mouthed another number, ending finally on seven, plus one in the driver's seat and another stepping leisurely out of the truck.

Dae-Ho could only see the man's feet as he approached and the tip of the rifle, which undoubtedly hung from his neck, swinging just below his waist. His dark-brown leather boots staggered and even swiveled, seemingly unable to find a straight line between the truck door and bushes ahead of him. Laughter and blend of voices followed the soldier's unsteady steps, something about *it's nothing* or *wait until we get back* but Dae-Ho was too focused to hear or more so understand. All he saw was in the scope of his rifle, all he felt was the trigger, and all he heard were the whimpers of a lost infant boy.

He couldn't fight them all, as skilled as he was, Dae-Ho knew he crouched in that position vastly outnumbered. That realization came with a cringe and a frightening thought that began at his chest and rippled through him as if each heartbeat felt like a raindrop and he was a puddle for it to ripple through. The panic surged through every part of him and he tried not to entertain this idea, yet soon found that it had already begun.

His finger unfurled from the trigger of the rifle, his palm slipped off the handle and he let it hang. He still tried not to think about it but the nightmare of an idea continued as his arm dropped to his side and the mere touch of his silencer seemed blisteringly cold. He flinched, the feeling still trickling down his spinal chord yet he somehow slipped the gun from its holster. He tried one last time to purge the thought from his head but it was too late. He wrapped the boy into under his arm and shoved the silencer into his mouth.

Dae-Ho heard a few muffled screams as the silencer rattled against the boy's few and still forming teeth. He in turn rammed the gun down firmly towards the his tonsils. The boy gargled, then coughed as his arms flailed and he tried to kick free. Finally the boy began to squeal just loud enough for the soldier

who stood no more than ten meters away from the bush to hear.

Dae-Ho heard a voice just then. A voice that sounded as clear as the men in the truck and child under his arms. The voice seemed familiar and like one that he hadn't heard in a long time, his propaganda conscience. Dae-Ho flinched as if an invisible tongue stroked against his ear and whispering, *"Pull the trigger."*

Dae-Ho's heart dropped and his trigger finger tightened. His finger seemed to splash against a trigger that felt heavier than its ever been for him. He struggled to curl his finger into a knuckle because now he finally felt it. He wasn't numb and he could taste, smell and feel every detail in the air around. He cringed his eyes shut and into a frill of wrinkles as he felt the bullet slipping from the muzzle like a premature or unwilling ejaculation. In the end he couldn't even watch.

After that there was nothing. All that remained audible was the engine of the truck in the background rumbling like the pant of a heavy dog. No more screams resounded, no more kicking nor whining echoed in the bushes and yet there was no muffled thwack of a bullet from a silencer. Only the sound of saliva could be heard, sliding against the boy's cheeks as he nursed on the silencer's long black muzzle like a lethal nipple, as if trying to suck the bullet out.

Then the sound of urine trickling onto leaves and settling into a puddle on the dirt and soon to be mud, brought Dae-Ho's attention to the soldier. The man sighed and spit and sighed again, until the flow of piss began to drizzle like leaking faucets onto his boots. Then as haphazardly as he came the soldier staggered back to the truck and his cohort's chuckles and chatter.

The truck pulled off immediately and dragged with it the thousand clanks and chimes from its engine, tires and beaten body and faded off like the last instrumental of a song on the radio, forever lingering. Lingering so long on Dae-Ho's ears that he felt the noise sounded like low humming earrings that just wouldn't stop, until eventually they did.

The boy still sucked on the barrel of the silencer, now more ardent than before. His eyes began to close and he found a comfortable position on Dae-Ho's lap. His last gesture before he fell asleep was to wrap his chubby fingers and thumb around Dae-Ho's index finger, which a moment earlier lay on the trigger of the gun.

Dae-Ho sat back and rested his shoulder blades on a stout plant that stood too short to be called a tree and far too tall to be a bush or shrub. As his lips popped open for a sigh he thought he heard himself speak but he didn't. What he heard was a voice, his propaganda conscience or some other ghost of his consciousness, whispering towards and about the gun placed inside the child's mouth and saying, *"I couldn't have put it any better myself."*

Dwain Worrell attended Georgia State University where he studied various forms of creative writing including screenwriting, poetry and fiction. After graduation Dwain became an instructor at New Oriental University in Beijing. During this time Dwain has published numerous short stories including: Fermi's Paradox for Black Matrix Publishing and The Little Things for Black Magnolias, to name a few. He has also penned the screenplay for the feature film: Walking the Dead. Dwain is currently the head professor of English Literature at New Oriental University in China.

Boy Sleeping
Michael Neal Morris

The boy is sleeping on the couch. It is
his turn to "camp out" on this, the last night
of Spring Break. Hours ago he fell off
the chair he was dancing in and received
a small knot on his forehead. Soon after,
his eyes were as bright as ever. I want,
as I recall the irretrievable
losses of the day, to hold him. As if
one could take the world inside a warm palm.

Michael Neal Morris has published online and in print in such venues as Borderlands,
The Concho River Review, Illya's Honey, The Distillery, The GW Review, Chronogram,
Mouth Full of Bullets, and Sniplits. A number of his books are listed at Smashwords. He
lives with his family just outside the Dallas area, and teaches Eastfield College.

A Long Way To Go

Roger Real Drouin

Under the clouds like gray broken plates. Here he was, chasing true scientific endeavor.

The photographer of birds hiked further into the 26,000-acre South Carolina pine bluff, the wind heavy with that wet coldness. The rain would be coming soon.

He knew he was chasing a ghost.

He hiked farther along the two-rutted park service trail. The rain would come within the hour, he thought, but despite the pale white-gray sky, it felt good to be in the field again. The strong coffee in his thermos and the new snug-fitting hiking boots were two modest checks in the positive column. From the boots to the cotton-canvas pants, and the thick flannel and heavy rucksack, the photographer was prepared for the weather, and the motion of the hike kept him warm.

He was searching for the Northern Stilted Curlew, one of the world's rarest birds, a species last documented in 1961. This arctic shorebird was what is called a grail bird—it may or may not exist. In Samuel's thick four-volume Master Guide to Birding, the Curlew was listed as "probably extinct." A color sketch showed the sturdy, dull-looking bird capable of flying the longest annual migration of any species, other than a handful of sea birds that can stop and rest on the water. Every September, the Curlew fattens up on

114

crowberries, worms, and insect larvae, before flying south to the end of the continent, logging in close to 10,000 miles on the flyway.

Just about every ornithologist and biologist in the world favored the more unfortunate outcome: the last Northern Stilted Curlew had decades ago made its final annual migration north to south.

Samuel heard the pine needles crush before he saw the two figures ambling towards him. He expected to see more birders along the trail, at least a few of those semi-retired, Tilley-hat-wearing folks who check the rare birds database on the web nightly. But maybe the weather had kept them home. Or maybe, most just reasoned it was not worth the trip. A less rare, but much more plausible sighting, such as the Kirtland's Warbler, or an accidental sighting of a species way out of its range, like the Cuban PeWee in South Florida, would draw dozens in pursuit.

Here in these pines forty hours earlier, an amateur had spotted what he *thought* was the Northern Stilted Curlew. This same scenario happens often.

An excited birder could easily mistake the long bill, dark brow marking, and the strong, rapid wing beats of the white-bellied, stilted Whimbrel for that of the cream buff-bellied, and slightly smaller, Curlew. From a distance, it's also easy to confuse the long stilted legs of the Northern Stilted Curlew to those of the Stilted Sandpiper. The Curlew's delicate pinkish buff under the wing, the decurved bill, and its unique call would be the most distinguishing features.

"See anything," he asked the couple.

"Nothing but a bunch of squirrels," the woman said.

The man wore pants and a Columbia rain slicker, a hunting style-cap, and a small hiking pack. The woman wore the standard, floppy Tilley hat, a thick fleece shirt, shorts with long socks above her old running sneakers. She toted binoculars and a Canon SLR around her neck.

"And a few Carolina Wrens and one Ruffled Titmouse," the husband added. "It's been pretty quiet."

"They'll be out when the rain clears," Samuel said.

"If it clears," the man said.

They knew he was here for the Curlew.

"We drove down from Connecticut," the woman said. They were die-hards, Samuel thought. "She was seen near here, not far, right?"

The sex of the possibly-observed curlew in question had been unknown. If it was in fact a Curlew, it would be difficult to distinguish the sex—both sexes look very similar, only the female is slightly smaller, and an immature can be mistaken for a female. It would be very difficult to determine if it was a female, unless the bird was seen up close. Samuel had written down the notification from the online Rare Bird Database: *Reported Northern Stilted Curlew…unconfirmed sighting… sighted at Darney Bluff National Preserve, four-and-a-half miles northeast of the main trailhead, directly north of the old hunting check-in station along a short loop trail. The bird was observed for thirty seconds before it alighted and flew in a north-north east direction.*

"The report said four and a half miles northeast of the main trailhead, directly north of the old hunting check-in station, which is about a mile further," Samuel said.

"We were out that far, near the check-in station," the husband said and looked up. "That thunder doesn't sound good."

So they were there, Samuel thought. That doesn't matter. If the Curlew was still in this pine bluff, it could be in the same area, but not the same exact location. After the rain, the Curlew would fly east towards the marsh and eventually back out over the Atlantic to its flyway. The bird was more than halfway to its wintering destination, and it wouldn't wait behind here while it had such a long way to go.

Scientists consider sightings of extremely rare species to be only hypotheses that require rigorous examination. A bird presumed by many to be extinct would be countered with disbelief, and scorn. For Samuel, a peculiar observation in the Everglades four years ago, combined with a list of other reports, formed his hypothesis that the species may not be extinct. There's a lot of space left from northern Canada to Argentina for a handful of birds to become nearly invisible. It may just be able to exist undetected by any of us.

Only true scientific endeavor could reject or accept his hypothesis.

He kneeled in the dark space, took the small tarp from his rucksack and folded it atop the layer of pine needles. He tilted the mug, sipping the last of the coffee, including the crunchy grind sediment the filter didn't catch. Some of it stayed on his tongue, grainy and bitter, before he swallowed it down. He put the empty thermos into one of the compartments. He took out the 200 mm long lens and clicked it onto his favorite camera, an older digital Nikon. The Nikon was a few inches bigger, and heavier than the newer models, and Samuel liked the sturdiness of it. He set the 300 mm lens on top of the pack where he could reach. The two plates of egg-and-bacon that he ate at the hotel would be wearing off soon. He took out two of the granola bars from the side compartment.

Waiting it out, leaning against the back of the old three-walled hunting station, he was grateful for the half-rotten, weathered structure that stood between him and the *ptttt plunk plunk* of the rain beginning to fall on the rusted roof.

He sat with his back against the shelter, his arms around his knees so only a few drops of the rain slanting down into the black soil splashed onto his boots. The wind came through in an unsteady whistle. It was high-pitched, silencing all other sounds, and then hesitant but rhythmic. Without the motion of the hike to keep him warm, the photographer of birds rubbed his hands together.

He ate the granola bar and sipped some water, and listened to the wind. Out here, he felt all right, cold but dry and sure that he was where he was supposed to be. He did not know if the Curlew existed. No one did. But here, once the rain cleared, he would continue to look. That is what he could do, and it is what he would do once the rain letup, which he could tell it would by that lighter shade of gray, the wind less cold and heavy. There were many things he had second-guessed, and maybe some of them he had once considered faith. He thought of everything he really had faith in. Some people had faith in things they grew attached to, or could claim ownership over. That wasn't true faith, was it? Was faith the very things that made us less reckless? He had a long time to think about religion, and he was still formulating his take on it, but he did have faith in God's judgment over man. And a judgment would come.

He did have faith in dreams, dreams that sank right down into the images and sounds of thought. He had faith in the memories of his dreams. The memory of his wife when she was disappearing in the hospital, and how she would smile in the middle of the pain when he walked in. That was some kind of faith she had. A friend had told him once that he could move on, try to meet someone new. His friend was only trying to help him.

Samuel thought about his son, how when he was just a boy, four or five, all he'd want to do is hide up in his closet and sketch giraffes.

"It isn't hiding," Lorine had said to Samuel. "The boy is living. Look at how happy he is."

Samuel worried because his son could remove himself from the world the way his father could. Lorine would tell him it was OK, their son was a beautiful, extraordinary boy, he was thoughtful and liked to draw, and if that meant he was a little different, who cares if he would rather spend the day sitting by a lamp in his closet sketching while every other boy on the street rode their bicycles in a pack.

She loved Ry so much, and maybe she loved him more because the boy had this different look in his eyes, eyes deep green like the different shades of a forest mixed all together. She loved the boy fiercely. She kept him grounded, but through her respect for him, she also kept him from changing. Even before he could walk, she idolized him. It was her idea to encourage him to apply to the new arts charter high school, and the scholarship to college. The boy was always thinking about his drawings, and in many ways he was just like his old man, but Samuel worried because he knew it would easier for the boy to imagine less and interact more.

And now, thirteen months after his wife's death, Samuel saw how his son was walking the way a young man would when he was detaching himself further from the world. He was walking like no one could see him. By detaching himself from the world he was inheriting, Samuel hoped that his son could stand it, at least get through all the scary parts.

He looked out, through the rain.

Once the clouds cleared, the pines would let squares of sunlight flow through. But now it was a pale darkness between blue and gray under the pines. The high-pitched *hak hak hak hak* came above the wind, from the east. He leaned outside the shelter to hear the Peregrine Falcon's coming from the top branches of a Maple tree about three hundred yards off. Placing the camera and tripod on the pine needles and adjusting the aperture to let more light in the lens, through the viewfinder it appeared—the bluish brown feathers and the dark gray malar stripe, and the broad wings tucked along his side. He snapped a dozen photos—some with the falcon looking down, or towards the shelter, and then a photo of the falcon staring sharply at the man with the camera before ascending at an angle a jet could never pull off.

He viewed the photos on the Nikon's screen, and zoomed in on the one gray and blue falcon that came out in perfect focus. In the winter of 98, under the grain towers in Superior, Wisconsin, he watched a Peregrine, only slightly larger than this one, pursue and strike a Ring-necked Pheasant. The speed and power of that Peregrine Falcon was remarkable. Pheasant feathers exploded from the pheasant when it was struck. It was one of the photos he was most proud of.

The rain had stopped, but the gray lingered. There would be no sun this afternoon. He packed up the rucksack, leaving out the camera, which he slung across his neck.

He hiked north on the park service trail, past the Maple the falcon had flown from. He looked up, and stopped every few yards to listen. It was his habit. His son said he always had his head in the clouds. He turned down the narrow singletrack east now. After a half-mile, he heard another call. But this stopped him in his tracks. It was a call he'd never heard before, a call from a bird in flight that he could not locate.

Samuel stopped and listened. He had been walking when he heard it, and he knew sounds heard while walking could be distorted. Please, let me hear it again, he thought. Please, fly this way. The only movement he made was inching his fingers to the Nikon, to feel that it was there. It was a sound that matched descriptions he had read, a sound that no one had ever recorded.

He did not hear the sound again. He listened, standing then sitting under the wrinkled trunk of a tall pine, looking up into the sky. He took his field journal and pen from his rucksack. With the journal to a new, unmarked page, he wrote his location as best as he could describe it, noting how far he was down the trail past the narrow creek bed and describing the pine taller than the other trees.

When he got to writing the sound, he found there was no exact language to describe it. It was a soft whistle—no not a whistle—that was the word that had been imparted in his memory from reported accounts of the Northern Stilted Curlew. In 1949, after the species was already decimated from intense hunting and disappearing habitat, Frank Kerrson saw a pair of Northern Stilted Curlews, and described their call as "a low tremulous whistle." Audubon, who had painted the Curlew for his Birds of America, described the call as a soft whistle.

Samuel scribbled and crossed out and then wrote: *It was like someone trying to whistle loudly but blowing air. Like that, but more musical. The bird called in series of threes in the same pitch, not more than three series, before all sound broke off as quickly as it came. I stopped in time to hear, without the distortion of movement, the last series of faint calls* **tee-teeee-teeee**.

He did not hear the sound again.

He listened, looking up to the rain falling again, the gray lacking light. He listened for the bird to call again. An hour later, he headed back towards the trailhead, still listening.

Rain dripping off his hat low, he walked past the perfectly still fox looking out from his den of green. The man's boot steps were the only sound beside the rain falling on the pines.

Roger Real Drouin is an MFA student in creative writing/fiction at Florida Atlantic University. His short stories have been published, or are forthcoming, in the print journals The Litchfield Review, Grey Sparrow Journal, and Leaf Garden and online at Pindeldyboz, The Smoking Poet, Northville Review, EarthSpeak Magazine, Canopic Jar, Madswirl, and Green Silk. His Web site is www.rogerdrouin.com. Roger also writes an outdoor blog at www.rogersoutdoorblog.com.

Parenthetically, before we start this story, there's someone you should be introduced to first. Meet Mr. J, a mouth-breathing-barbaric-lousy-writer so self involved that he failed Astronomy 101 because he literally thought the world revolved around him.

Mr. J is in the midst of writing a new book or as he called it *"an Amish blog"*. Chances are it will be total flop and have more unread pages than a crack dealer's beeper while on sabbatical. Mr.J was a black robe and sickle away from being language's Grim-Reaper. Mr.J was to language what hemlock was to Socrates, what Pontius Pilate was to Christ, what Lee Harvey Oswald was to JFK, and what Rush Limbaugh was to credibility of Rush Limbaugh. Understanding Mr.J's style of writing was like solving the Rubik's Cube...color blind.

For the next chapter of his book, I mean his *Amish Blog*, he's constructing a top ten list of hebetudinous however helpful hints to delineate if you are demonically destroying decent discourse. As if you were an allegorical Aerosol Spray Can eliciting global warming on the Proverbial Planet Pretentious Pedantic Pomposity as it orbits in the Semantically Snobbish Solar System:

1) -You think "Barnes & Noble" is a description of a fancy farm.

120

2) *-Spell check has no suggestions other than "Don't expect people to read this."*

3) *-Your favorite author is a guy named Cliff Notes.*

4) *-You think sweat shops make deodorant.*

5) *-You never order a Caesar Salad because you're afraid a Brutus and Claudius Salad will stab it to death.*

6) *-Someone said, "I'm watching Ripley's Believe It or Not." And you reply, "I believe it."*

7) *-You think Olive Garden should open an adoption agency because when you're there you're family.*

8) *-In your mind, Books for dummies describe all books.*

9) *-You can only speed read with books on audio aka press fast forward and use your book mark aka pause button.*

10) *-Face book is the only book you've ever read.*

Incidentally, this particular story is not about Mr. J. No it's about a murder of his closest friend who of course in Mr.J's case was a stranger. His name was M.T. Jester, a fuzzy fellow that looks like the love child of Chewbacca and Sasquatch. Hair dragging behind his feet like a Bride's dress that makes follicles of Repunzle on Rogaine seems as if it's the smooth skull of Lex Luther after leaving the barbershop. This Cousin It carbon copy, known as M.T., is a professional unicyclist who could only do one trick: a wheelie. He was sponsored by Neosporin.

Now that we've met everyone; Let's rewind one week, to last Tuesday, where this story begins, okay? Alright, so...it's last Tuesday and it's a crisp calm night, as the velvet twilight glistens and gleams from sparkling silver pepper stars sprinkled across the powdery air of the black tarp hovering overhead restlessly. And M.T. is busy in his looking for his new titanium shovel so he could clear a space in his yard for a glow-n-dark sundial.

Suddenly a stealthy silhouette wavers through the shadows. Sneeringly the silhouette emerges clutching the missing titanium shovel in his nervous hands that are quivering like Michael J. Fox during a game of Jenga. The mysterious figure strikes M.T.'s cranium, cracking completely open as if it's a piñata full of dark rose colored blood. Exactly one week later on the subsequent Tuesday-a week after the attack and M.T. lies on his death bed, pale as a winter moon. He's forcing an awkward smile before sinking into the unknown abyss of afterlife. Nostalgically he reflects on past events in life such as his freshman year in college when he tried speed dating. Not on purpose, he was just dumped a lot.

As death lurks nearby it seems almost as if a heightened sense of M.T.'s sparse source of mortality is plunging over the ragged edge of the universe that was once crimson lit full of youth giving air. More reminiscence consumed him with memories of when he was 18 and lost his virginity followed by memories of being 19 and realizing he didn't lose it but simply misplaced it between his low self esteem and social awkwardness.

Eventually everything surrounding M.T. becomes sinisterly desolate dreary and dark. His universe was becoming cold lifeless and absent of all short winded elations. Eyes closed so tight as he grasped at insignificant concepts for comfort. Turning over in his mind how he displayed such amorous feelings towards light savings time because he loved jet lag without packing.

And who else other than the fetid sump-sucking, Mr.J would be the last person privy to M.T. Jester's final uttered syllables. Most of what he said to Mr.J made as much sense as a mime performing ventriloquism or a dyslexic playing

boggle or buying a coffin with a lifetime warranty.

Mr.J, yawning feigns interest with a camouflage of affectation as his neighbor rambles, rants relentlessly. Musing amphigories such as *"Cannibals truly are what they eat."* And things like, *"The early bird gets the worm so if you're a worm, I'd sleep in."* Or even, *"If the alphabet was one long word, it would be easy to spell but hard to pronounce."*

M.T.'s fluttering lips. Banality of banter flourishes nonsense like a Blue Angel soaring through social-stratosphere. Caroming off intergalactic solar plexuses of vastly vacant headed vernacular that's so boring even his tape recorder was now just pretending to listen. It was a cheap Sony

Handheld Recorder: batteries and attention span not included.

Suddenly, M.T. stifles, truncating his jostling jabbering jowls and becomes quieter than a librarian with laryngitis for several moments. This of course abruptly elicits Mr.J to regain intrigue. By this point Mr.J had begun playing on his laptop which was full of Trojans, viruses, and never worked. Essentially his laptop was Lindsay Lohan.

Mr.J's eyes glance around the room and involuntarily fasten in awe with M.T. who returns a blank ambiguous stare. M.T. conveyed a familiar conviction as if he was a magic 8 ball during an earthquake: Answers would be easier to understand if someone asked a question first.

Silence consumes the entire room and shattered as M.T lightly interposes and whispers in a husky tenor with great trepidation and Mr. J leans forward with eagerness. Moving wistfully before him hesitantly unveils his only veridical secret. An ancient mystery so old it makes Alexander Graham Bell's prototypes look like the new iPhone.

And, M.T. fragilely murmurs:

> *"I have a confession. You never knew this. But, I've been secretly having an affair with your girlfriend."*

Wicked words from a wicked tongue poison the ear and resonate to the deepest crevice of his stitched skull. Mr.J pauses, motionless, reticent, reserved, and statuesque. The air is rich with tension and dramatic turbulence that builds at a steadfast and unwavering pace and is released.

As Mr.J smirks and replies contemptuously:

> *"I have a confession too. I already knew about the affair. And, that's why last Tuesday night, I borrowed your shovel."*

Mr.J is currently working on 3 new novels, a joke-a-day calendar, and submissions for media. Mr.J is also featured in USA TODAY reporting his achievement of the coveted "BEST BREAKTHROUGH AUTHOR 2011 AWARD" presented by the reviewers and staff of UK's underground publishing house, Indie-Press, INC.

REP

Lynn Kennison

Lilly noticed the whispering glances when Kyle—captain of the football team and the most popular boy in the senior class—winked as he passed her by. She smiled shyly in return. His attention was not something she was used to. Their association had been somewhat arranged. For Kyle needed to pass algebra to keep his position on the football team, and Lilly—who is a junior and already acing calculus—was asked to tutor him. In the afternoons, she would drive over to her algebraic deficient friend's house, where day after day, Kyle would answer the door in a sweat dampened t-shirt, gym shorts, and a dirty ball-cap covering his darkened dirty-blond hair; but all of this was easily overlooked as Lilly peered into his mesmerizing blue eyes sitting across from her. Before that wink, he hadn't much acknowledged her during normal school hours.

At lunchtime, Lilly took her usual seat across from Ben—her loyal best friend and fellow socially inferior classmate. She knew the look on his face all too well. Lilly has known him since they were eight-years-old, and one of his good traits, is that he has always been a really bad liar.

"What do you know that you're not telling me?"

"I don't know anything. I'm just eating my lunch," he replied with his eyes down—one of his surefire giveaways.

"Yeah.....well you just ate a carrot." The carrot being another clue, because Ben had always hated carrots. "See, something has your preoccupied....so....what is it?" Lilly pushed.

Ben hesitated at first, but then leaned closer and whispered, "it's about *you* and *Kyle*."

"What about *me* and *Kyle*? I'm tutoring him; you know that."

"Yes, but I've heard a rumor that after you tutor him.....well he kind of tutors you."

"What? What could Kyle possibly tutor me in....he has something like a 2.5 GPA. Besides football, he's probably only interested in one other..... " Lilly's words trailed off as she looked at Ben. "Who has been saying that?" she demanded to know.

124

"Kyle has. Matt heard it from Casey who heard it from Monica who heard it from, I think, Daniel who said he overheard Kyle telling Sean in the locker-room after practice yesterday."

"Well I don't care what Matt, Casey, Daniel, or Sean heard or said; it's a load of crap!"

"And Monica…."

"Ben, that's not the point important here." Lilly didn't like the way he is was looking at her. "You think it's true!"

"No I don't!" Ben exclaimed in a pitch higher than his normal tone.

"But you thought about it, and If my own best friend believed it then…."

Lilly wondered who else would think it was true as she looked around the cafeteria. She became somewhat paranoid when she noticed a few glances followed by chatter. Her face began to boil as she spotted Kyle laughing over at the popular table—seated amongst mostly football players and a few cheerleaders and prom queen prospects.

She turned back to Ben, "Okay, it doesn't make any sense. Why is he over there and I'm over here if we're supposedly….you know….together."

"In his words, he's just teaching you a few things you could stand to learn, and that's it."

"What!"

"I'm just repeating the words I heard," Ben defended himself.

"Why would they listen to him?" she scoffed.

"He's pretty convincing." Ben said before dodging a hurling carrot.

"You're supposed to be my best friend Benjamin!"

"I am! That's why I told you….so you could do something about it. Confront him and stop tutoring him. He deserves to fail."

***

That afternoon, Lilly arrived early and waited patiently on Kyle's front porch trying not to reflect on the rumors going around. When she saw his black pick-up pulling into the driveway, she managed to keep her composure. They headed for his room. His expression became perplexed when Lilly unexpectedly slammed the door behind them.

"We need the privacy for my lesson, right?" she asked sarcastically.

"Oh…"

"Yeah, I heard. Why did you say those things?"

He flashed a cavalier smile, "Oh come on…..it's not like your social status hasn't improved since we've been hanging out. So what if I embellished a little bit? You should be thanking me."

"Thanking you?" Lilly was taken aback and appalled by his arrogance.

"Weren't you tired of being invisible? Now people are wondering about you. Plus I think I know how you feel about me."

Lilly couldn't believe what she was hearing. At one point, not so very long ago, she may have had a tiny crush on Kyle—okay maybe more than just *tiny*—but now she was

125

relieved of all her underlying symptoms by the insulting, presumptuous, cocky bullshit that spewed from him.

"Tomorrow, I'm telling everyone what a pathetic liar you are," Lilly said and abruptly turned to leave.

"No one will believe you." He called out.

Lilly pulled her hand from the doorknob and turned back to face him, "I think something in your brain is loose. You can't just expect that people will go by your word alone."

"Come on Lilly, who are people more likely to believe? Me, captain of the football team, third year starting quarterback, most popular guy in school, or...." He trailed off.

A lump began to build in her throat as she fought the urge to cry. Speaking for the moment was out of the question, for the tears would have surely betrayed her. At the same time, she fought the strong urge to walk over and punch him.

"This works out for the both of us really. I have a reputation to uphold, and now you finally have one," he said.

Realizing that some of this was partially true—sadly more people might choose popularity over brains—Lilly dropped her gaze.

Kyle's mother tapped on the door and popped her head in. "Sorry to disturb you kids, but I just wanted to make sure Lilly was staying for dinner."

Before Lilly could answer Kyle answered for her. "Sure she is Mom; Lilly loves your cooking," he said as he put his arm around Lilly's shoulder.

"Oh good," Kyle's mom said before exiting.

When the door was shut, Lilly elbowed Kyle in the ribs and shoved him. He fell

126

backwards onto his bed as he laughed.

"Get out your algebra book," Lilly demanded.

"What?" Kyle asked.

"Well, I have a rep in algebra to uphold, so you need to learn a few things before I leave," Lilly said.

"I knew you would come around."

"Just stay on your side of the bed," Lilly said as she helped Kyle with his algebra one last time.

***

Friday finally came and everyone was getting ready for the big rivalry football game including the starting quarterback, Kyle, who had just one more thing to do—pass his algebra exam. He managed to sneak in his notes he copied from Lilly, to cheat his way to victory, and finished the exam in record time. With a smug expression, he handed in his test and asked to be dismissed early for the pep-rally.

In the locker-room, Kyle was talking to two of his teammates about the game. Their attention was diverted to the door as their coach came in. He informed Kyle he didn't pass his algebra exam, and effective immediately he was on academic suspension. Kyle couldn't believe it and argued it was a huge mistake! There was no way he got any of those answers wrong! Suddenly, he realized that Lilly must have sabotaged him.

Kyle found Lilly standing outside the auditorium waiting for the pep-rally to begin and rushed her down a nearby corridor.

"You did it on purpose," he said in an accusatory tone.

"Did what Kyle?" Lilly smiled innocently.

"You know exactly what. You gave me the wrong answers, so I would fail my exam and get kicked off the team."

"Well at least now it looks like you *really* haven't been using your study time wisely, right?"

"You're going to tell the coach the truth right now."

"You mean he won't take the word of his starting quarterback. Well that doesn't fit into the world according to Kyle, does it?"

"Okay, I see what you're doing. Are you done having fun yet?"

They were interrupted by one of Kyle's teammates Cooper. "Hey Lil, you left this in the computer lab," he said as he handed a notebook to Lilly.

"*Lil*?" Kyle questioned.

"Thanks Coop," she said.

"Are you coming to the game tonight?" Cooper asked her.

"Hey man, fuck off, will you? I'm trying to have a conversation here," Kyle intervened.

"That was a little harsh," Lilly said after Cooper walked away.

"Well forgive me if I'm not in the jolliest mood. Will you tell the coach or not?"

"Fine," Lilly answered.

Lilly's revelation did not work out how Kyle had hoped—or how Lilly had expected for that matter. Because of their conduct, both parties were punished. Lilly was suspended from the next math-team match, and Kyle wouldn't be reinstated on the football team until he retook the algebra exam and passed it.

As they walked out of the dean's office, Kyle asked Lilly if she would be going to game.

"No," she answered, "you?"

"Nah."

They walked quietly for a moment. "Do you want to come over," Kyle asked.

"Sure," Lilly shrugged.

Lynn resides in the sunshine state. She makes her home with
her husband, their four dogs, and a fat, lazy gray cat.

Joe Farley

Shadow & Light

in the light of a broken sun
shadows and cold wind bring no hope
of flowers exploding with red,
a life only of white and gray.

tomorrow's song will fall flat
in no atmosphere for hearing.
listen to the vacuum of time
and human incandescence.

seated cross legged in a space suit,
visor of helmet pulled down,
escape from this kingdom of shadows
and find inside the sustaining light.

Joseph Farley edited Axe Factory for 24 years. His books include Suckers, For the Birds and Longing for The Mother Tongue (March Street Press).

More Than A Mouthful

Joanne Faries

Tony swept the beach with his Geiger counter and concentrated on the steady click, click, click. Then, clack, clack, clack, the staccato double beat of a winner. He stopped, dug with a shovel into the sand, and took a minute to pocket some change. Not quite a dollar's worth, but a decent haul. Tony sang aloud, butchering his favorite Jimmy Buffett song "Cheeseburger in Paradise." After a final chorus, he turned off his machine, wiggled his tan toes in the sand, and calculated his early morning effort at almost ten dollars, not to mention some sea glass, a Casio sport watch, and a Frisbee. The song made his stomach growl and he glanced at his cell phone to check the time. He could hit the boardwalk, afford a monster lunch, and then stroll to work at Mack 'N Manco's.

An ocean breeze ruffled his blond hair and made the new fuzz on his arms and legs shiver with goose bumps. He ran a finger across his upper lip trying to decide if he had a mustache yet. Fifteen was so futile. "I'm nothing. Oh my seashore goddess," he called out to some seagulls swooping overhead. "Mary Ellen Castellanoto." He shouted her name and it muffled in the wind. Gulls squawked and Tony's ears heard "sucker."

 Layers of clouds in the distance built a wall and the sun now hid. Normally near noon the beach would be festooned with colorful towels and lazy bodies. Tony inhaled but there was an absence of suntan oil today. Predicted rain and the stormy deep green surf did not beckon. Instead movies, arcades, and the pizza joint would be jammed as bored vacationers dodged under the awnings and sought entertainment. He chatted at a crab scuttling towards the water. "Might as well go to work and at least look at girls. Busing tables makes me invisible." He collapsed his equipment and stuffed it in his backpack, but decided to wear his sunglasses as a shield from the wind.

Jogging on the wet packed sand, Tony veered away from the water to the boardwalk. He churned along, his large feet flipping sand behind him. At the stairs, he slid on his Adidas flip-flops. Taking the steps two at a time, Tony decided on a double-double burger/tot combo. He ambled over to Gino's stand, placed his order at the window, and attempted to flirt with the cashier. She rolled her eyes as he dropped sandy coins on the counter. Greasy bag in hand, he smiled thanks and asked for extra ketchup. The girl turned her back to answer Gino's phone and jot down an order. Tony stood for another second, shrugged, and then hurried to nab a bench facing the ocean.

Tony liked to watch storms roll in. He sprawled on the seat so he could view both the water and the boardwalk, wave or talk to a few friends, and wolf his lunch. Most guys were late to work, so no one lingered to beg a tater tot or kill time. Chewing, Tony projected himself into the future, hosting an end of season beach party. He'd have a bonfire, kegs of beer, and tons of girls, like Mary Ellen, in bikinis. As owner of Mack 'N Manco's, he'd have way more fun than his father. "Hell," he thought, "if you're gonna live at the beach, you might as well make it worthwhile." Tony shuddered, picturing his father's pale stork legs poking out of swim trunks, and the ubiquitous socks and sandals. "So not cool." He took a huge bite just as a group of giggling girls sauntered past.

Sitting up straight and swallowing whole, Tony nodded. "Yo, Mary Ellen," he squeaked. Mortified, he shrank back into his seat, and then watched as a petite redhead, who he recognized from school, peeled off from the pack to speak. "Hey, Mr. Clueless. Mary Ellen's mine." She reached over and popped a tot allowing her lips to form an "o" around it before actually taking a bite. Walking back to her group, she turned her head, puckered, and blew him a kiss.

Speechless, Tony sat and processed this information. What chance do I have in this town competing with lifeguards AND cheerleaders? It's hopeless. With that, there was a whoosh of wings, and Tony was left with remnants of greasy paper smeared with mustard. "Half a cheeseburger gone? You gotta be kidding me," Tony groused. "Compete with the damn seagulls too."

Joanne Faries, originally from the Philadelphia area, lives in Texas with her husband Ray. Published in *Doorknobs & Bodypaint*, *Off the Coast*, *Orange Room Review*, and *Salome* magazine, she also has stories and poems in *Shine* magazine, *A Long Story Short*, *Up the Staircase*, and *Freckles to Wrinkles*. Joanne is the film critic for the *Little Paper of San Saba*

Michael Sauvé

"The whole magic universe is dying."
William S. Burroughs—*The Cat Inside*

Somebody once said, "A screaming came across the sky," and it didn't seem to mean anything except it sounded cool. But then a screaming *did* come across the sky and you started to wonder if maybe that guy knew something all along, starting such a giant book with that one line of terrible prophecy.

When other spirits try to lock on you can sometimes seize up. I had to close my eyes. I felt like someone wanted to process information through me, because I was a technical writer and I could express the messages. This projection said I'd get it all down as my memories came either chronologically or not, regardless of tense or presence of fact. It would be the essential document of the shadows that fell across the world. I wasn't a medium but I knew how to meditate. I could hear the third-person voices. I'd always heard the third-person voices and they'd made me shiver right before sleep.

March 1

Shortages of fuel, water and supplies led to the panic. The anti-gouging laws lasted only as long as the rule of law, which wasn't long at all. Criminals stormed the retailers and grabbed what they could when the social order showed its first cracks. The first grisly images began appearing on the news: a little girl trampled, an elderly man in a wheelchair mugged in broad daylight, a woman gang-raped while horrified spectators looked on helplessly. My parents own an isolated piece of farm property with a deep well. I hope they are on it.

I worry most about families, their loved ones who are missing and the communication problem. I can't get to a phone and mine died at the start. My Internet works only through the cable; something is disturbing the free Wi-Fi you could once depend on in the city. The social networks are full of gross distortions now. Apparently they were all for some sinister purpose. Images of corpses are sometimes uploaded as Profile Pictures....those images are haunting every time but the future.

I worry what will happen once the spotlight turns off. If we get past this crisis we'll have to accept a new standard of normalcy, and then the second wave will bring us down even lower.

My mood was lightened briefly by an email from my boss saying my services wouldn't be necessary for the foreseeable future. She assumed I would otherwise have been in the mood to commute several hours through the riotous streets to teach an already meaningless Microsoft Excel lab. I'd never likely see my boss again so I queried her on an End Times E-course I might put together. I ended my email by saying, "For the time is at hand." It seemed funny to me but my services were flatly declined.

March 6

The CIA's MK Ultra mind-control program had recently revealed Lady Gaga as their mind-controlled slave in a surreal press conference on MTV. Media had focused primarily on the war in Israel since the formation of the state of Babylon three years earlier. The Gaga announcement happened a solid week before any other weirdness so the press had a difficult time digesting it, immediately labeling it a publicity stunt. Then members of secret societies started to make pronouncements that they were and always had been the true controllers of the earth. Their video press release showed massive supplies of diesel fuel and dried food, so I was convinced. But it wasn't anyone well-known so the media gatekeepers denied these doom-criers also.

Rumours surfaced that on top of the rioting, the shortages, and the earthquakes there was a World Health Epidemic of mania and contagious rape instinct, a total release of the suppressed genitality of the blocked-up masses. Internet commentators suspected Lady Gaga's organization at first. The rape disease was later identified as a strain of the aggression virus that started in the prisons. The jails were a fertile breeding ground for the great anger. It can be traced back to prisons all over the world. I think that's important to note.

A man calling himself Himmler emerged who looked an awful lot like Heinrich Himmler, but he was discredited by the press because he did not look exactly like Himmler. Nonetheless he became a leader among the various Aryan militant groups throughout the United States and mobilized them as one unit. This was never on the news at first. The Islamic terrorist groups were the preferred scapegoat and received considerably more airtime, but terrorism was merely a pleasant diversion by then. No one was gathering in stadiums or flying on airplanes anymore.

March 8

Down the street there was a car crash, and then it happened again just as it had happened before. The very same cars and people arguing. The second set of people did not appear conscious that it was a repetition. "Come see this," I told my wife. She shook her head and I could see the goose-pimples on her arm. It was the first time she would admit that a rational-material worldview could no longer apply.

City workers mysteriously appeared to fix a broken water main. City service had been suspended as far as we knew. We had still been able to get a slow drip of water out of our faucets and flush the toilet but once they finished we were bone-dry. I had watched them deliberately cut off our water.

It was dangerous to leave the apartment for water so we decided there wasn't enough for the dogs to drink. We had to let them go because we didn't want to watch them die that way. But they didn't run away. They stood outside the door of our apartment building looking scared. It was my responsibility to let them go because my wife couldn't do it. We lived on the second floor and when I got back upstairs we could see them barking at the front door of our building in a panic. There wasn't going to be any food or water for them outside either. They were too domesticated. They would get scared and turn vicious. We couldn't do that to them so I went downstairs and let them back in. But we gave them less and less water and they whined all the time.

Marijuana and alcohol consumption were untenable causes of dehydration, so I couldn't even dull my senses. The cable lasted longer than anything so we were always up to date on the horrific daily developments. Before the unraveling I'd have never believed I could enjoy cable news without weed and alcohol.

March 10

I thought the earthquakes might stop but they didn't. A large aftershock hit close enough to us and broke all the windows; by some dumb-luck we had a large piece of fiberglass we were able to block the main one up with. For the first few days we'd only watched the earthquakes on the coasts. When the CN Tower fell we stood by the window and watched. A bright green mist in the air couldn't be identified. Once it came in through our smaller windows we started going crazy.

I considered my brain and how much blood it would require to continue operations. No longer did I feel autonomous but that my physiological functioning was in the hands of some mysterious syndicate. They didn't owe me the steady flow of

134

serotonin I was accustomed to. No one neurotransmitter can stay in fashion forever.

March 12

I came to love every sip of water. We had filled several four-litre jugs from the drip and rationed as much as we could in the beginning, but that barely lasted a week. We finally ventured out to buy jugs on the black market that had sprung up on George Street where the crackhouses were. The crackheads must have known something; they'd started hoarding water early and now they were on top of the economic spectrum. I'd bought drugs on the street before so I thought I could bargain with these guys, but I only got 20 litres for $600. Half a litre a day each for the arbitrary period of 20 days. I suggested going back for more before the violence increased.

"I can't," she said.

"I'll try."

"You can't go alone."

She was right. We'd barely made it back with this haul after the incident with the old man. I was trying to stay in control of my emotions because I felt these could be our final days. I tried to love my wife, but the love-feeling did not come natural as it once did. Facing all this horror our emotions should have stirred. We'd always loved each other almost like a brother and a sister. But a new coldness had spread between us, caused not by these new stresses but by the new condition.

March 13

The commercials were still on TV for insurance companies that said, "When you love someone you'll do anything for them." It seemed to me that commercial time should have been commandeered by some emergency management agency. Better yet would have been a highlight reel of human achievement, to give us even the goodbye treatment of a long-running sitcom. At the very least they could have used the time for a few good jokes, like Bukowski saying in bone-dry desperation, "We have wasted history like a bunch of drunks shooting dice back in the men's crapper of the local bar."

The hungry and homeless masses continued fighting over supplies. Tens of thousands tried to leave the city each day. "Unacceptable" the acting Mayor called it, but it was really something to see, a pretty vicious-looking exodus. Particularly nasty things happened to some Swedish hockey players.

Their attackers were the first confirmed cases of the *accelerated* aggression-rape

135

virus. Until then the rapes were officially attributed to the breakdown in law and order, but these attackers were convulsing, and certainly raping with a new level of malevolence. The images of the castrated and desecrated Swedes were the end of hope for even the most optimistic Internet commentators.

No one had been beamed up to heaven by God either. Many evangelical Christians were discouraged that they had not ascended. The true believers were undiscouraged, believing as always that they would meet God in death. Both groups were convinced that tribulation was well under way.

March 15

The Himmler videos on YouTube became my primary fascination. A creepy bald female medium named Destini had predicted the return of Himmler in a YouTube clip from 2001. She predicted many things however, so rational-skeptics argued she was bound to get something vaguely right. They didn't want to admit it was the reincarnation of Himmler anyway. It was too familiar. The mystical blood cult of the so-called "Aryan race" originated with the fortuneteller Madam Blavatsky. She was nothing but a cheap con and they killed six million.

March 17

The American cable landscape quickly incorporated all sorts of wild figures. Alex Jones' (a fringe radio host and conspiracy theorist par excellence) wild predictions had been proven accurate and this became a legitimate news story. Alex Jones replaced Larry King when Larry King was killed in one of the earthquakes. He began his broadcast, "The moment is at hand...

"It is spreading through sexual intercourse, most often forced, and it was started by these MK Ultra sex slaves, like Lady Gaga has already been exposed as on PrisonPlanet.com. We have been telling you this was coming for years and now it is here. It has been independently confirmed by *The New York Times* and countless publications.

"The President has been exposed as the fraud we always knew he was. There is a Reptilian race with the ability to shape-shift among us, and a half-breed, human-Reptilian species. Many of your beloved news anchors have already been exposed. *[Images of Greta Van Susteren, Eliot Spitzer, Jon Stewart, Glenn Beck, and John McCain appear in background]* Human DNA has been mixed into these creatures, programmed if you will. This involves programs like MK Ultra, CIA Black OPS, and basically every dark force we have described on PrisonPlanet.com. For this collaboration with lizard people you have sold your souls forever! I only hope it's not too late.

"We told you what they were doing. Now you say protect us from these all powerful operators. Well...we are mobilizing on the *new* CNN social networking site as we speak. There is a group on Facebook but I urge you not to trust it. This is vitally important so I'll repeat that: You can no longer trust Facebook, or any of the major social networks. They have been taken over. Any Alex Jones content you see on

Facebook I can assure you is coming from the global elite and is intended to misdirect and fragment our constituency."

He continued like this. In the other camp were the less television-friendly quantum philosophers who believed that Jones, David Icke and the other conspiracy nuts had somehow manifest their own desired reality. Certainly what they had proposed couldn't have been true until it became true. All of their claims had been thoroughly discredited. But then they came true.

A man showed up at CNN's Atlanta studio and said to Alex Jones' production assistant, "Hello I'm Brion Gysin." He looked identical to the artist and provocateur Brion Gysin, who was said to have shared a third mind with William Burroughs (Burroughs writings were enjoying a renaissance in these times). Gysin was inventor of the cut-up method, inventor of the dreammachine, and a general dandy who died in the 1980s. Nobody that important, but someone who had said some strange, upsetting things in his life.

They asked how he'd returned and what the score really was, but he yawned and said he didn't want to talk about it. He just wanted to repeat some lines he'd used before.

"Ask me what we're here for," he said.

"Why are we here?" asked Alex Jones.

"We're here to go."

"What could we have done differently?"

"'Rubbed out the word.' As Burroughs informed us, 'Word begets image and image is violence.'"

"What do you mean?"

"The narrative was running into the ground and it could have been halted. They dropped an atom bomb for Christ sake. But you couldn't make people stop thinking, or talking, or expressing dangerous ideas, or thinking about death. You couldn't stop Timothy McVeigh, and that should have told you something. You couldn't stop Lee Harvey Oswald either. These were not anomalous men; they were part of a calculated system of chaos. This system grew exponentially in power as information sped up. These kooks with their misspelled blogs became as relevant as the *Wall Street Journal*. We should have known where we were headed after we saw the look in Oswald's eyes; we should have put a computer on the job, not left it up to lazy, stupid man."

That was Brion Gysin. The only other recorded interview he gave during his brief resurrection was a long hostile diatribe against Gore Vidal. Then he seemed to disappear altogether.

It was followed by a 20-minute segment on Himmler, now increasingly prominent in the new mainstream media due to his massive military gains. He suddenly had fortified compounds throughout the American south. The segment consisted of material taken largely from his YouTube page.

Jones ended his broadcast with a clip of an evangelical preacher named Jeffrey Gant whose End Times message had become increasingly popular since the start of the war. "I read to you from the book of John: 'Little children, it is the last time: and as ye have heard that antichrist shall come, even now there are many antichrists; whereby we know that it is the last time."

This was the very first *Alex Jones Show*. It was kind of cool to sit back and watch it all go down at first. As a student of the cable landscape, it was interesting to see it stretched beyond capacity, and then simply continue in its new paradigm. This was a welcome diversion from our current issues: lack of water and untreated injuries...which themselves were just a preview of what was to come.

March 18

We had to let the dogs go. We weren't laughing much after that. You couldn't flush the toilet and it was starting to stink, and they were pissing and shitting up the place. This wasn't the issue; the issue was the water, but if we'd have known how close it was to the end we'd have kept the poor guys. We really loved those dogs. They looked scared again, but this time we hid our heads under our pillows for a long time and when we finally looked out the window they were gone.

It had been so ugly when we got the water we did. I'd nearly been robbed on the way home. I was cut with a pocketknife by some determined old man who'd tried to steal our small cart. Now that wound was infected. He'd probably lanced his hepatitis-oozing boils with that knife. He was almost 80 so I threw him to the ground easily. I gave him a hard kick to the gut and didn't regret it one bit. How we made it home without getting robbed by a more dangerous entity I'll never know. We wouldn't be so lucky a second time.

There were no longer any organizations to provide help. A disproportionate number of civic officials were dead. Chaos seemed to be spreading chemically and with purpose. Across the world the earthquakes had been precise, leaving hardly a government building or hospital intact. The news networks were the only sector operating near full capacity. This could not have been coincidence.

138

March 21

Now the moon is almost invisible in the mist. The fortunetellers have totally taken over the A and E Network. There is a sudden awareness that every point of view is significant. The realm of imagination is now as real as a pretentious formula. Folklore is relegated to reality. Art is no longer content to occupy any kind of frame.

Everyone is either holing up or else fighting like animals on the street; there are no good Samaritans despite their existence in literature; there are no carnivals. No performances of *Othello*, just fear. No 21st birthday parties, just rape attacks and group rape attacks.

The God consciousness is spreading among a segment of the population; more and more people perceive themselves to be God, or part of a consciousness system that is God. This isn't so far from the good old Christian message. But this is just one side of a two-pronged occult attack. The other side is the cult of self-interest which emerged in the 1990s: "I'm the director of my life. I'm special," is the essential motto, but they were the same as anyone else, just men facing a great flow of vengeance.

March 22

We understand things in terms of mechanism, but not theory of mind. My dream will be as important as observable mechanics...and my dreams have become increasingly operatic in scope lately, beacons of hope. I'm beginning to think this is a matter of false belief. Our brains are not binary machines. They are radios.

March 23

What will happen to our pages of white whales and green lights gleaming on docks; our prose, tender and ambiguous; Midwestern virgins in the shower, spied on by a slimy but otherwise loving stepdad after his ravenous crystal meth hit; the night air on a highway; the tearful laughing euphoria of a life-shortening whiskey hangover in the rock and roll morning? Where will it go? Tell me there's a God in heaven.

March 25

Am I a harlot writing a strange beast? What can these symbols mean? It really was the most important book in the world. It did reveal the future of humanity, the future of our earth, devastation to mankind, a white horse, a pale rider, a conqueror...because people read it, and believed it, and the schizophrenics knew.

I hope this is clear. My wife keeps nagging that I've got the schizoid-virus that's spread since last Sunday. Personally, I feel fine. My thoughts are clear and each one rings out like a bell to me. I feel my thoughts are crystallizing in this time for a reason. It's possible my wife has the rage disease. We've been having sex often despite the coldness I mentioned. Some can sublimate the rage disease into sex with an accommodating partner.

I'll get on with what happened. The crazier people were killing their own children and using their body parts in brutal sex-rituals. Those without the virus had the fear so bad they were shooting first and asking questions later. Something had to happen. It was John Stossel who bore witness then; most of the big-name anchors had taken themselves out of the game. We heard the voice of the fourth creature on CNN, "Come and see," and we beheld the graphic of a pale horse, and on it was a graphic of death. I recognized the beasts. I felt a sorrow because I'd wanted to go to heaven.

Two were ordinary men. One was less ordinary in that he had iron teeth. The other, a charismatic European General, was the political figurehead.   He had won the Nobel Peace Prize two years earlier for his role in the inconsequential Israel-Babylon peace talks. He was the persecutor but that was not obvious. He was only a man of sin, which cable audiences were accustomed to. It was the time of the absolute end and these beasts seemed like fitting characters.

The third and fourth beasts were actual beasts. One had ten horns. Men who gazed upon them were said to change. It didn't matter if you saw them in reality or on television. The fatally-wounded were made well for a moment, and everyone on earth marveled at the new beasts. They worshipped them knowing they were unbeatable and would solve the shortages. It was an inevitable, necessary transmutation, and a curse on us all.

March 26

I had ears but I did not listen. I was doomed to be captured and the people came when it was that people started breaking into apartments and houses. They axed down the door. We'd been watching the beasts on television and not thinking much about the aggression diseases.

140

They raped my wife many times and then started putting the knife into her. They pissed on me and told me I liked it. They stayed for two days doing this kind of shit. This evil had always been with us, all this time.

I wanted badly to mock them but it only made them more violent, but I still found it hard to resist. They were two burly old bums with jail tattoos.

They had a 14-year-old boy in handcuffs. He was treated better, but also abused sexually. They cut him slowly, with a sick fascination, while we watched. They were building up to the big moment when they fucked him together and beat him to death. They had a lot of meth-amphetamine and Viagra so they had erections all the time and all they wanted to do was fuck and cut us up.

They cut off my wife's hands because they thought that would make them feel something after many hours had gone by but they were disgusted with the result and killed her because she couldn't stop screaming. I told my wife I would pray for her soul but she couldn't hear me. I hoped someone would pray for my soul. They looked at me like a pathetic dog and one said, "Ah get out of here you faggot." But the other didn't want to let me go so easy; he told me if I could make him come I could go. He just sat back on the chair. He'd ejaculated dozens of times in the last couple days and it took almost two hours; the other guy kept cutting at me the whole time but I finally got the job done and out the door.

Expelled into the streets, activated into the gridline structure, my entire pre-programmed life spread out; shivering with the bloody asshole blues I'm brought into a collective of beast-worshippers right off the bat. They saw me and knew the score. "Have you heard the message of the great benevolent beasts? They have come from below where they've been waiting. They are here to restore hope." I thought of my wife for the last time. The machine was recalibrated in such a way that the followers of the beasts could see in a new way. I could no longer see in the old way.

Anyone who refused was alienated, essentially left to die. This world will have meant nothing in the end. A man can outlive his own heart, but not his own brain; this was the dream now fully interpreted. I went with them because I'd heard the beast camps were well organized with plenty of food and water for those who'd sign the ledger and receive the mark. I felt untold terror to see life beyond life. I could see their features, and the agony and the pain and the frustration that would lie ahead. The beasts were creating great illusions and we were absorbing them like deep healing breaths.

A graduate of Ryerson Journalism, Mike Sauve has written non-fiction for The National Post, The Toronto International Film Festival Group, Exclaim Magazine and other publications. His fiction has appeared online in Rivets Literary Magazine, Forge Journal, Candlelight Stories, Straitjackets Magazine, Eastown Fiction, Foliate Oak Literary Journal, the humour journal Feathertale and elsewhere. Upcoming stories will appear in print in Palimpsest, Infinity's Kitchen and Kitty Snacks.

To The Crying Venusians

Sergio Ortiz

My skin shrieks,
a cave dweller notified
of yet another death,

I did not want to leave
a trail for redheaded dragons
with fiery tongues to terrify

empty lighthouses,
meadows, and the jingles
of readers on my day
of resurrection.

Queen Lazarus unwraps
my feet with the grace
of a deer tutoring my hands
in the art of dying.

Daddy, daddy, daddy
my knees are skin and bone.

I wear a pink triangle
and numbers tattooed
around my ankles.

*Ortiz is a retired educator, a poet, and photographer. He has a B.A. in English literature, and a M.A. in philosophy. Flutter Press released his debut chapbook, **At the Tail End of Dusk,** in October of 2009. Ronin Press released his second chapbook, **topography of a desire**, in May of 2010. His photographs have been published or are forthcoming in: W5RAn.com, The Neglected Ratio, and The Monongahela Review. He was recently published, or is forthcoming in: The Battered Suitcase, .CRUDO, WTF PWM, The 13th Warrior Review, Mad Swirl, and Heavy Bear.*

Another Day In Paradise

Stephen Frentzos

"This day can't get any worse," Daniel Riley, twenty-six years old and four years removed from college, muttered to himself as he exited the subway car and ascended the staircase. On the top step he once again greeted the gray, dreary Monday evening in Boston whose appearance exemplified Daniel's mood at the moment. It had been a trying day, indeed, one that was filled with so many unpleasant developments that Daniel would have struggled mightily if he were asked to classify it as either a mild tragedy or a comedy of prolonged misfortune. But he was almost back at his apartment now, and as he saw the ragged, dirty old homeless man slumped against the exterior of the train station rattling a plastic cup filled with coins in his direction under the gloomy, dampened autumn twilight, Daniel thought back to the morning when his anguish started.

*   *   *

The alarm clock blared out its incessant, irritating call, a nervous, high-pitched, periodic scream that continued at a frantic pace until Daniel rolled over and slapped the snooze button to quiet it. When he later stirred again, he was immediately startled by the inauspicious silence permeating his bedroom. "Please, not again," he thought as his heartbeat began to quicken.

It was a little over three months ago when Daniel's alarm clock first decided to ignore his request for just a few more minutes of slumber, refusing to shriek back to life even after he had firmly pressed the snooze button. And then it happened again six weeks after that on a morning when Daniel vowed to himself that he would purchase a new clock that evening. But he had returned home from his job as a financial analyst late that night, weary from his day at the office, his exhaustion compelling him to trust the old, worn device and forget about its former acts of defiance. The alarm clock had performed flawlessly since then, but today it had chosen to once again play its deceptive, spiteful game with Daniel, and as he saw that he had slept an hour longer than he had intended, he leapt out of bed.

After brushing his teeth, combing his hair, and throwing on the first blue dress shirt and pair of tan trousers that he could tear from their metal hangers in his closet, he grabbed his briefcase and ran down the stairs that led to the rainy street from his apartment building, sprinting toward the train station in the midst of the precipitation.

Along the way, as Daniel was concentrating on the stream of cars approaching the intersection that he was trying to cross, he stepped down from the sidewalk into the middle of a large, cold puddle that swallowed both of his feet.

"You should have watched where you were going!" an overweight man in his forties with gray, thinning hair and an amused grin on his face chuckled to Daniel through the slightly opened window of his white electrician's van that was stopped at the light beside where Daniel stood.

"Thanks, that's very helpful," Daniel mumbled under his breath before he darted across the street and down the stairs that descended toward the subway.

Daniel crept into work that morning in his soggy shoes and socks, wary of alerting his colleagues of his tardiness by traipsing noisily past them. He was satisfied when he had successfully traversed the short row of cubicles leading to his desk without drawing the curious stares of any of his fellow employees as he scurried by, however his stomach dropped as he noticed the note scribbled on a small sheet of yellow paper stuck to his computer monitor. "Please see me in my office when you get in," it read, and it was signed by the vice president of the company, George Macklin.

Daniel's shoulders slumped as he crumpled up the note, threw it in the garbage can next to his desk, and trudged dejectedly toward George's office like a captured soldier being led from one prison camp to another.

Daniel took a deep breath before knocking on George's door and opening it a crack. "Mr. Macklin, you wanted to see me?" he said timidly as he stuck his head into the office.

George lifted his vision from the report he was holding and nodded once he recognized Daniel. "Yes, please come in," he said as he dropped the report on his desk. "Have a seat, Daniel."

Daniel sat down in one of the two brown leather chairs facing his disgruntled superior. He was nervous, and his uneasiness only intensified as George studied him in silence.

George was an imposing presence with his tall, wide frame, short, thick silver hair combed neatly to the side, expensive, custom-tailored black suit and rugged, creased face that proclaimed to Daniel that he had no doubt encountered several problem employees in the past and possessed very little tolerance for their insubordination. He leaned forward now, resting his arms on the dark, shiny mahogany in front of him as his body loomed commandingly over the desk. "You're an hour late," he announced finally, his words sending a pang of

discomfort streaming up Daniel's spine.

"I know, Mr. Macklin, and I'm sorry, but -"

"This is the third time in the last three months that you've been late," George interrupted, his tone rigid and unforgiving. "Obviously, you feel that this job isn't important enough to show up at the appropriate time for."

"No, Mr. Macklin, that's not it at all, I just -"

"Because let me assure you, Daniel, that our financial firm is one of the most prestigious in the country, and the integrity that echoes with our name is personified by everyone in this corporation. We have no place for someone who betrays that integrity, who makes up his own hours and blatantly disobeys the strict standards that we have set in place to ensure that our company remains a model of proficiency. Now, if you plan on being even a minute late from this day forward, don't bother coming in at all, because you will be terminated. Mark my words, Daniel."

"I understand, Mr. Macklin. I'm terribly sorry."

George then glared at Daniel for a moment longer before he picked up the report he had been reviewing and turned his attention to it. Daniel welcomed the gesture, felt relieved as if George had just mercifully turned off an enormous burner that had been lit beneath Daniel's chair for the last five minutes, and

145

scampered out of the office and back to his cubicle.

Daniel labored without pause for the remainder of the afternoon, even forgoing lunch, the one gleaming oasis amid the endless desert trek that was his job, to complete the work that had sat idle on his desk during the hour that he had missed that morning. When finally he was done for the day, having loaded his briefcase with various files and documents only thirty minutes past five o'clock, his usual time of departure, he stood and started walking toward the elevator when he heard Deborah Finn, his direct supervisor, a woman who Daniel had grown to despise for both her shrill, irritating voice and her habit of pointing out any errors he committed that she came across while reviewing his work in a demeaning, derogatory manner, called out his name.

Daniel froze, the warm, comforting image he had of his apartment, his home, his haven from the anxiety of the outside world, fleeting from his mind. He lumbered over to Deborah's cubicle. "Yes?" he asked, annoyed.

"I was just looking over your income report and I noticed one of the figures you used is wrong," Deborah whinnied. "See here," she said, pointing to one entry in a column of numbers, "this should be a thirty, not a twenty."

Daniel grabbed the piece of paper she was holding and examined it. "You're right. My finger must have slipped when I was typing it. I'll correct it first thing tomorrow."

"Actually, the client needs this report tonight. And this number is used in seven of the calculations you implemented later on in the report, so you're going to have to change those as well. You know, you could spare the both of us a lot of hassle if you used more care when preparing your reports."

Daniel closed his eyes in aggravation, the rage churning inside of him threatening to seep forth from his mouth at any second. He regained his composure and said, calmly, "All right, I'll fix it right now."

It took Daniel twenty minutes to revise the report, and when Deborah had approved of his amendments, he raced from his office to the train station, eager to get home as soon as possible.

When the subway arrived at the platform, Daniel was enthused to see that, as he had been trapped at his cubicle for the majority of the rush hour bustle, the train was nearly empty. He sat down at the very end of the last car and exhaled his frustration in one long, soothing breath. Daniel began to get lost in his thoughts when an elderly woman gripping a small paper cup filled with coffee sat down a seat away from him. She smiled gently in his direction before she removed the plastic lid of her beverage and blew on the warm liquid that reached to the rim of the cup.

Daniel watched in dismay out of the corner of his eyes as the train eased to a start, jostling the woman and causing a few drops of coffee to spring free from the cup and land on the fabric of the seat next to him just inches from his thigh. His stare became fixated on the cup as the woman gradually lowered it closer to Daniel's leg while the train charged forward. With every sudden increase or decrease in the vehicle's velocity, Daniel's eyes widened as he watched another wave of the brown liquid splash on the seat perilously close to his trousers.

He looked at the woman, her eyes closed in blissful ignorance of the tumult she was creating. "Just take a sip of your coffee!" Daniel felt like screaming at her. "Or at least put the lid back on until you're ready to drink it!" But the woman just sat there in silence, peacefully enjoying her ride.

As the train pulled into the next station, Daniel had just decided to switch seats as soon as the subway stopped moving when the elderly woman opened her eyes and stood up. Daniel sighed, grateful that this form of psychological torture was over, and relaxed his shoulders. It was at that moment when a short, aggressive man boarding the train surged recklessly through the doors, colliding with the woman and sending the contents of her cup directly onto Daniel's chest.

Daniel didn't flinch when he felt the tepid liquid soak through his shirt,

 didn't even raise his head as the woman apologized before stepping off of the train. His day had already been discouraging enough, his spirit filed down to nothing more than a jagged splinter of indifference by the adversity that he was forced to contend with for the last several hours.

That mentality lasted for only a brief amount of time before Daniel saw Pamela Baker sitting across from him a few seats to his right. Pamela, looking more strikingly beautiful than ever in her short black skirt and tight lavender blouse, had been Daniel's girlfriend for two years until she ended their relationship eleven months earlier. She had told him that she fell in love with someone else, a man named Robert who she met in one of her classes at the graduate school she was attending, and the news had devastated Daniel. He had adored her, savored every minute they spent together, and during the ensuing weeks after she had broken his heart, Daniel fought with all of the strength that he could muster to prevent falling into a state of depression, a feat he accomplished with the help of his friends and family. He hadn't spoken to her since the day she left him, hadn't seen her even though they lived only four blocks apart, and now that she was less than ten feet away from him, Daniel didn't know quite how to react to her presence.

Pamela, sensing that she had elicited the steady focus of the man closest to her, ventured to look in his direction but promptly averted her gaze when she noticed it was Daniel sitting there with his concentration fixed squarely on her. She turned her head away from him, clinging to the hope that somehow he hadn't seen her glance at him, but that feeble bit of optimism disappeared almost instantly.

"Hi, Pamela," Daniel said, his pulse quickening, his face void of expression, his words sagging with the forgotten sorrow that he was suddenly reminded of by the sight of Pamela.

"Oh…hi, Daniel" Pamela replied uncomfortably, coercing her lips into a reluctant smile. "I didn't see you there."

"How are you doing?"

"I'm doing well. How has everything been with you?" Pamela asked, her absorption straying to the large, unsightly coffee stain that cloaked the front of Daniel's dress shirt and extended down across the zipper of his pants.

Daniel's face reddened as he followed her gaze, remembering the incident that the shock of her appearance had thrust into the furthest recesses of his mind. "Obviously, I've been better," he answered sheepishly.

"I think I have some tissues in my bag if you need them," Pamela offered without hesitation, shedding her former apprehension while she reached into the brown leather purse resting on her lap. She stood up once she found a pile of napkins and walked across the aisle, sitting down next to Daniel as she held them out to him.

"Thanks, I appreciate it," Daniel said as he began dabbing his chest with one of the napkins. "I don't know what it is, but I just can't seem to catch a break today."

"You know, now that we're here, I'm actually glad that I have this chance to talk to you," Pamela announced as her eyes met with Daniel's.

Daniel stopped patting his shirt with the napkins. "Why is that?" he asked as he peered into Pamela's familiar, kind green eyes.

"Well, I still feel awful about the way things ended between us, and I regret leaving you so abruptly. You were always a great boyfriend to me, and you didn't deserve any of the pain that I caused you. I realize now that I was too immature to appreciate everything that you did for me. I was lucky to have you, and I have no doubt that you're going to make some special girl truly happy. So, I just want to say that I'm sorry for everything, and it would mean a lot to me if

you could one day forgive me for what I did."

Daniel took a deep breath when Pamela was through speaking, holding the air in his lungs for a moment and then letting it out slowly through his nose. He then shook his head as a slight grin formed on his face. "I forgive you."

"You do?" Pamela blurted, surprised.

"Yeah, why not," Daniel affirmed. "I mean, what good would it do me to stay angry at you?"

"That's such a relief," Pamela gushed as she grabbed Daniel's hand.

Daniel glanced down at her hand on top of his, felt a pang of energy course through his body, looked back up at Pamela, and asked, "How are you and Robert doing, by the way?"

"Actually, we broke up eight months ago."

"Oh, really?"

"Yes, unfortunately. He wanted to get married right away and I told him I wasn't ready for that kind of a commitment."

"I'm sorry to hear that," Daniel lied.

"It's okay. We never really connected on an intellectual level like you and I did. I have to admit that sometimes I wonder where you and I would be today if I hadn't acted so irrationally when we were together, but I guess that everything happens for a reason." Pamela then looked out the window behind them as the train pulled into the next station. "This is my stop," she then said, standing up.

"Hey, Pamela, would you like to go out sometime?" Daniel stammered hastily as the doors opened. "Maybe we could get a drink later this week."

"I'm sorry, Daniel, but I have a new boyfriend now and I don't want to jeopardize what I have with him," Pamela replied, cringing her face as if she was delivering a fatal diagnosis to Daniel. "Take care," she said, and with that, she stepped out of the car and onto the platform.

"That's just perfect," Daniel murmured as the train sped forward again.

*   *   *

And now, as he stood there gaping at the poor, morose homeless man extending his cup of change toward him in his dingy, faded green flannel shirt and ripped brown pants that were heavy with the weight of the rain that he had been exposed to all day, Daniel retrieved his wallet from his back pocket and removed a twenty-dollar bill from its folds. "Your day was worse than mine, I'm sure," he said as he stuck the twenty into the cup.

The homeless man quickly recoiled his arms, peered down in disbelief at the bill hovering almost divinely over the shallow pool of pennies, nickels, and dimes, glared back up at Daniel with a look of astonishment, and exclaimed, "God bless you, sir! You're a true saint among men!"

"Use it for the right reasons!" Daniel advised as he scurried into the street.

"I will!" the man called after him. "You don't have to worry about that!" As Daniel continued down the sidewalk that led away from the train station, he heard the man still yelling behind him, "A true saint among men!"

Stephen Frentzos grew up in Massachusetts and graduated from Boston University. He currently works as a fund manager in Boston. He loves to read, and his biggest influences are Kurt Vonnegut and Cormac McCarthy.

Boothbay Harbor
Joe Taylor

So, it's morning in Boothbay Harbor, Maine, a gentrified town that has lost its soul. I want a cup of coffee. Just regular black coffee and maybe a hard roll and butter, or what they call a bulkie, like I used to get mornings years ago while working in New England. The only place I can find is a fancy dancy upscale deli on a pleasant hilltop overlooking town with baroque gilded patio chairs and a better than thou attitude. I tell the phony ass woman behind the counter that I want "just a regular black coffee". She looks at me like I've just asked to abduct her seven year old granddaughter and points me, with condescending finger, to their "breakfast blend". And then goes totally "nose in the air" when I attempt to explain the concept of butter on a simple hard roll. My only other option being a nectarine scone. I purchase the coffee and relent, out of hunger, to the scone and evaporate, as she would have me, from the deli's hallowed walls, thinking it interesting that she finds my currency less objectionable than my breakfast order and my obviously pedestrian personage.

Later that evening after a cup of hearty chowder, a platter of tender fried scallops, a half dozen beers, and some good conversation with one of the few remaining locals to run an establishment that is not a tourist trap, I find myself walking the now deserted streets of Boothbay Harbor. I am inhaling my cigar and the beauty of the town sans visitors and want a place to sit for awhile and take in the serenity of the moment. What better place than from the patio of the locked and empty hilltop deli.

Ah, the tranquility of a picturesque town at sleep. Ah, the urge after six beers to pee. Ah, the answer, to check out the deserted streets for a patrolling cop car. Ah, the relief as I empty my bloated bladder onto the source of my morning's humiliation and its fine baroque gilded patio chairs. Ah, the satisfaction.

After a lifetime spent in broadcasting, Joe Taylor has retired to the "woods" of rural northwest Pennsylvania where he is rekindling his enthusiasm for self expression, which he did successfully on the radio, and attempts, at great risk to himself these days, as the only openly liberal patron of his friendly neighborhood redneck bar.

What will it take for me to learn?
Never seeing hope in future;
Only in the moment;
This in reality doesn't mean shit.
I have nothing to live for;
I don't want to live for myself.
I'm on a road that never ends,
Walking with no destination;
Alone in a rusted cage with rats devouring my external
    existence;
Nothing matters.
How many self manipulated deep seeded wounds will it take
    to get to the center of my turmoil?
How much torture do I have to consume?
When will I be hypothetically full?
I'm just the carryon;
Life is the overhead;
I won't fit;
Like the missing piece to a puzzle;
It's gone.
I'm gone.
My conjunction of thoughts shut down.
I put up with the self destruction;
Do I love it secretly?
Maybe I do.
Maybe I love the pain;
If it's not obvious enough, Ha.
I love destroying myself;
At least I can't say I've never loved anything!
Lay me down;
Cut me open;
Dig at me with a wooden spoon;
Take out the hatred;
Feed it to me again.
The taste sounds oh so morbidly sweet;
I'm satisfied from the anguish.
Taste it again.
My emotions lathering my insides;
The fundamental object is to choke myself with the
    misfortune of my being.

Positive Thinker
Megan Elizabeth

Megan Elizabeth. Young, vibrant, dark and twisted. A free lance artist with talent coming out of her ears. Born in Worthington, Ohio in the year of 1988, she began to first express her emotions on paper when she was old enough to hold a pastel. Since then she has had many accomplishments, including a state young author award and an art internship. If your interested in going deep into a troubled mind this is your girl.

152

The Last of The Paramours

Phyllis Green

Since I was the serious child and also the oldest at eight, I could calmly talk to my mother as she packed her suitcase in preparation of leaving us. Sally, the three year old, was crying and blowing her nose into Mother's knees. We ignored her.

"But why?" I asked again, for her answer "because" hadn't satisfied me.

She plopped bras and underpants in the brown plaid case. All white. No lace. She wasn't a lacy girl, me mom. She was skinny and had no butt to speak of. Her skirts wrinkled up. Her blouses were always half-out and askew. Her nylons sagged. She was messy. She had long hair—well, shoulder-length. Mine was so short, anything seemed long to me. Mary was her name. Me mom.

"I'm going to go off with Alicia. We want to kiss and sleep together and Daddy wouldn't like that," she said.

"I'm sure he wouldn't mind," I said. As you can see I really didn't know much at eight. I was also thinking of myself. Yes, I was eight but clearly that was too young to become head of household. The dreaded brothers would drive me batty. Gerald, seven. Bobby, six. And Andrew, eight months. And all my mother thought about was damned Alicia. I sucked my thumb for a few seconds and then announced,"We shall get along

without you very well. In fact we shall thrive." Oh, my eight-year-old vocabulary and oh, how wrong my prediction.

In the years to follow I packed school lunches, washed diapers, asses, faces, and hands, picked up toys, did the boy's homework, burped Andrew, patted Sally's head, cleaned toilet seats, picked up clothes, and was the general nanny even though Daddy helped here and there and hired ladies to do cleaning and other chores on an irregular basis. But I was the glue. And if the others didn't thrive, at least I did. Gerald and Bobby flunked fourth and third grades. Sally broke Andrew's leg. Bobby's birthday cake burned in the oven. Sally got third degree sunburn and we all got measles, mumps, and chicken pox. Gerald shot a neighbor boy's eye out with his BB gun. Andrew's leg was set wrong and that's why he limps.

All the boys when they turned fifteen, as if it was a requirement, got girls pregnant. Sally smoked and got a tattoo and nose ring. I was there listening to their troubles, consoling. Good old Jessica. They could always come to me. I never blamed it on Mom leaving. It was the times. Darlings, tell me all about it. Jessica will make it all better.

Daddy scooted me off to college and I studied to become a teacher. And then one day I saw her again. Mary. Me mom. I was behind her at the grocery checkout. I was nineteen and she didn't know me. But I recognized her right away. She looked the same age as when she left but now she was hanging on to a man, caressing his cheek, laughing

softly. It appeared she was now kissing and sleeping with him. I did not introduce myself. I felt no bitterness in fact I felt nothing but surprise.

Also I didn't want her asking about us. She didn't need to know that Gerald was serving time or that Mitzi, the part-time waitress, part-time lap dancer had moved in with Dad and only wore a pink towel around the house and had moved in her Barbie doll collection and had her brown and white pony tied in the backyard. And the fact we all liked Mitzi. She was a breath of fresh air and also she never tried to upstage me with the kids. She let me be Mother Teresa even though I was at school and not home all that much. Mitzi was fun. Laughter finally rang out of the house at 310 Villa Verde.

The house had become a bit of a dump but I loved it. It was a fake Tudor and the furniture hand-me-down and mix-and-match. Beat up rugs smelling of cat pee. Candy green walls that needed new paint. A blue and white-checked kitchen tablecloth. But oh, it was home. It felt like home. There was no place like it. It embraced me and gave out

warmth like a beloved baby blanket. Dad said to me once, "You love this house, why? What is there about it that gets to you? You bloom here." I loved that house and I meant to have it, when Dad was done with it of course.

I graduated from college and Mitzi left Dad for a cowboy. Bobby collected firearms. Gerald was out of reform school and in his first marriage. Sally was on Prozac. Andrew was growing pot amongst the day lilies.

I taught retarded children in a nearby town. I knew I couldn't make them brilliant but I could make them wise, loving, aware, and safe. Eddie could dance the hula when we put Hawaiian music on the recorder. Mikey practiced writing his name for hours until his

fingers ached and grew calluses but he printed his name to fourteen valentine cards, his goal. Annie learned to set a table and fold napkins. Terry cried when it rained. I believed the atmospheric changes gave him real pain. Or perhaps it scared him. He once lay down on a trestle as a train roared over him. His mother told me that. Rain. Train. Did it have to do with that?

Eddie, Mikey, and Annie had the mongoloid features. I taught them that they were beautiful and handsome and I called them by those names. Terry, Donna, and Nancy were labeled autistic and in the not too distant past experts had blamed mothers for this condition. But I knew the mothers. If that had been true, Sally, Gerald, Bobby, Andrew, and I would be autistic. That's why I smiled at the mothers and dished out successes to tell them so they could feel good.

I taught these children to say no to sexual predators and yes to true affection. I brought in experts in self-defense and got advice from psychologists and books on how to protect feelings against verbal abuse because often words could do more harm than punches. They learned the symbol for poison and the sign for railroad crossings. We went shopping for food and learned to make change. We got on a bus and paid the driver. We planted flowers and marched through art museums. We went to farms and zoos and band concerts. My troops and I. We

studied dinosaurs and stars. Addition and subtraction. And I read them great stories.

Before I knew it I was thirty-eight, still teaching, still single, still in my little schoolteacher apartment. All three brothers were married with children and respectable jobs. Bobby was a policeman. Gerald, an electrician, and Andrew worked for Gerald. Sally had her nose ring removed. She was a beauty and modeled Pendleton woolen dresses and slacks for catalogs. At home she spray painted tire chains in pastel colors and wore them as decorative belts. She felt the fashion world would soon follow in her

footsteps. None of us had won the Nobel Prize but we had survived and become responsible adults. Then Dad got ill, very ill, and everything changed. Somehow Mary got wind of it. Mary. The mom. And she came home to nurse Dad.

I waited a week and then I visited and already I could see Dad was besotted with her and so were the other kids. I wasn't keen on the way she parceled out Dad's medicine so I said very gently, "We don't do it that way." She gave me a look. I knew that look. It said, "Now, we do."

It was suddenly clear to me. She *had* seen me in the grocery when I was nineteen and ignored me. She hadn't left thirty years ago for the drama and heartbreak of romance but because of me. What was there about me at age eight that made her run away?

I knew Dad would leave the house to her. She would live there with her various paramours be they man, woman, or beast and when she died the last of the paramours would inherit my beloved house.

I slipped into the kitchen and took the dishes off the table then I folded the blue and white jelly-stained tablecloth and refolded it until it got as small as I could make it, not small enough to fit in my pocket but it stuffed nicely into my jeans and gave me the look of ten extra pounds. One small part of the house would be mine forever.

Phyllis studied Creative Writing with Lawrence Hart at the College of Marin. She is a graduate of Westminster College, New Wilmington, PA and the University of Pittsburgh.

The Last Word

It's hard work being the head monkey of a magazine. I mean, I know I have to sit around looking cute, but sometimes, there are tough decisions to be made. Look at this issue – over a year in the making, instead of the scheduled six months.

Why? Well, without boring you with details, let's just say that there aren't many aspects of the mag that have stayed the same since the last one. Those of you who have been reading for a while probably noticed the binding right off, and the thickness. We've just about doubled in size since last time!

As for the stuff you may not notice; there's a new printer being used (to save all of us money!), and because of that, we had to be a little more hands on. Good thing I'm a monkey and have four of them!

And, the delay wasn't all bad – aside from bringing you all the best issue of Ink Monkey Magazine ever, we've improved everything, and we've expanded into a small press. Before, we just considered ourselves a magazine, but now, we are looking forward to amazing anthologies, super special secret projects, and being a million times greater than we were before. (If you want to thank me, please remember I'm a

monkey. I'd much prefer a bunch of bananas to a bouquet of flowers, although I doubt the editor would agree!)

It wasn't all hard work, though. This past year, we've made some awesome friends – check me out with Nick Valentino's really cool steampunk props (don't worry, it's not a real gun!). Oh, and in incredible news, we made two important debuts this past issue – the Southern Festival of Books in Nashville, Tennessee, and the geek con circuit, thanks to The Incredible Stephen Zimmer, who started taking Ink Monkey with him, starting with MidSouthCon. (Where this issue will make its public debut, too!) If only I could get to go to all these cons, too! But, that's okay. Oh, plus, we brought in our first ever co-editor for this issue. We're looking at making it a regular feature of the magazine; who wouldn't want to guest edit something as cool as this? Phew! I'm getting tired just telling you about it all.

Anyway, it's been a long year. Let's not forget what was going on a year ago. And, you know, forgive us (again) for the magazine taking so long – we spent lots of long, sweaty hours cleaning, rebuilding, building, painting, clearing, etc, for those around us. Nashville has (mostly) survived its Great Flood, but there's still a lot to be done even now. We were incredibly fortunate that it wasn't worse for us, and we owed it to our city to give back to people who couldn't say the same.

While we splashed around in the front yard taking pictures, we had no idea that our friends were across town being evacuated by boat. Luckily, we all came out okay, and I'm more than happy to announce that the city has rebounded in ways that would put a smile on this old monkey's face if it wasn't stitched on already.

Remember the old cliché – That which does not kill us makes us stronger. After this year, we're strong as oxen (and we smell better!). We survived, and we're only looking at bigger and better Ink Monkey things on the horizon from now on. Until next time... Lots of happy reading!

Love,
Minkey Marie

www.ingramcontent.com/pod-product-compliance
Lightning Source LLC
Chambersburg PA
CBHW081209170626
46811CB00010B/3228